NICHOLAS EFSTATHIOU

KILLERS
in their youth

NICHOLAS EFSTATHIOU

KILLERS
IN THEIR YOUTH

Publisher: Dead Reckoning Collective
Book Cover Artwork & Design: Keith Walter Dow
Editor: Jessica Danger

Printed in the United States of America

Library of Congress Control Number: 2024934023

ISBN-13: 978-1-963803-00-6 (paperback)

For my wife, Carol, who helped me find my voice.

PUBLISHER'S NOTE

When we talk about what we take from the wars and from military service, we mostly talk about ourselves. The unconditionals and the forgiving ones standing by us are sometimes the ones affected the most by our experiences at home or abroad. Our families are watching, sometimes helplessly trying to do whatever they can to help us. Sometimes it's too much and our household bursts at the seams and another broken home pairs nicely with Veterans Affairs benefits. There are solutions and better ways. We get to choose how we present ourselves to the world, but if it's all a facade then eventually it will fall down, or things will slip through the cracks and into the fibers of our daily lives. The worst part of that is the next generation could perceive it as normal and carry on "because this is what my parents did it," no different than putting a Christmas tree up in December.

The crucial theme in Killers is not that these men and women experienced these horrible things and spent their lives trying to hold it together. It is the young observer we see in Ken, soaking in every story, reaction, and opinion from his father, his father's friends, and other members of his community who went to war. Ken is raised by a loving father and a strong community who wish the best for him, but there is something to be said about the filter or lack thereof used by them as they impart all of this knowledge to a young Ken. The characters in this book came back with guilt and shame, but they also came back with fear and hate. All of these are dangerous things to hold on to, but we can't just lock them up. We sweat it out, and it will infect our most precious, impressionable family members if we're not careful.

Different war, same story. So many of us come home angry, lost, and slighted. We don't even need to massacre a village in a foreign country because we come home firing in all directions at our neighbors. We say they don't understand, but make no attempt at helping them to do so. At best, we make one attempt and give up so we can say we tried, but did we? Are we trying? This story is an attempt, but it's not the first, and it won't be the last. This story serves as a reminder that if we come home carrying these things and fail to unpack them, we will be doomed to live a life full of hate and negativity. If you are battle worn already, these things will not lighten your load.

Our experiences and behavior can be like second-hand smoke for the ones we love who want to be near us, and it can drive them away or infect them even more severely than it does us. The more we look into caring for ourselves, the more we are looking out for the ones who depend on us and not just so we can continue to provide for them, but so that we don't pass on these negative character traits and afflictions. Generational trauma is real, and if we ignore our own issues, our children are the ones who will ultimately have to pick up the bill, and the cost may be more than the coming generation can pay. We should demand accountability for military action at home and abroad, and we should demand adequate care for our veterans when they return. But more than that, we should demand proactive approaches from ourselves and our peers. Our busted up bodies as temples and the lives we have left are the most precious gifts even at their most difficult. Be good to yourself and be better to each other.

This story is for the ones who came home and never stopped operating at a cyclical rate of fire. It is for the ones who were trained to never ask questions and then never shake the habit. It is for the ones who came after these ones and accepted "this is the way we have always done it" and "you would feel like that about them if you were there too" as gospel. It is for the ones who will go after, and it is also for the ones who won't; they might be the ones who need to understand this the most.

COLONEL ELBRIDGE ESSEX

"Where are you goin', Kid?"

Ken looked up and saw his father standing in the doorway to the kitchen. The man's dark hair stood up in a tangled wave, his eyes painted with exhaustion. His father held a mug of coffee in one hand and stroked his mustache with the other.

"Outside," Ken answered.

"No cartoons?"

Ken shook his head.

"You get your homework done?"

"Yes."

"Packed it away? I don't need you getting chewed out because you forgot to bring it to school again. Be a hell of a way to start the week."

"No," Ken assured his father. "It's in my backpack."

His father sipped at the coffee, absently brushed some out of his mustache and yawned. "Okay. Don't be too long. Got to hit the store before the Pats game time today, right?"

"Right."

His father smiled, turned, and the conversation was finished.

Ken opened the door to the apartment and descended the twisted, narrow stairs to the first landing. He glanced in the open door of the Cristo family's apartment and saw Mama Cristo standing at the small kitchen counter. She sang in French, which Ken didn't understand, and pulled open the jerry-rigged chicken-wire doors on the cabinets. Her hands, despite being twisted with arthritis, slipped in beneath her chickens and deftly removed the eggs the protesting birds sat upon.

As she put the eggs into a basket on the counter, she saw Ken and smiled. She called out a greeting in her Haitian patois, and Ken returned the smile as he waved. The old woman gestured to the eggs, and Ken nodded. Her smile widened into a grin, revealing her broken and stained teeth, and then she returned to her humming.

Ken continued his journey to the bottom door. The hinges complained as he pushed the door open, and Mr. and Mrs. Cristo looked up at him, lit cigarettes in their hands.

"Ken, good morning," Mr. Cristo greeted. "How are you on this fine day God has given us?"

"I'm good," Ken answered.

A single beam of sunlight pierced the porch roof and illuminated the old and weathered Bible that lay open on an upturned milk crate between the husband and wife.

"Would you care to join us in prayer?" Mrs. Cristo asked. She wore a black scarf around her head, and Ken knew she would never take it off. Henri, their ten-year-old son, had been killed by a drunk driver the year before.

He had been Ken's friend.

"No, thank you," Ken told her. "Do you need me to do anything for you today?"

Both of the Cristos shook their heads.

"Thank you, though, Ken," Mr. Cristo said. "We are fine today. Please, tell your father hello when you see him."

"Okay." Ken waved and went down the steps. He paused, adjusted the old army hat on his head. Battered and worn, it had been a rare gift from his grandfather, and one Ken refused to give up, despite its ragged appearance. Ken slipped his hands into the pockets of his jeans before he walked around the back of the apartment building. From the street beyond, he heard the occasional car, and in the yards behind the building, younger children yelled and called out to one another as they played.

Ken didn't like them. They had always been mean to Henri and to Ken for being friends with him.

Crossing the cracked pavement of the parking lot, Ken went to the old carriage house. The doors on it were secured with new chains and padlocks courtesy of his father. Ken had been caught roaming around the rotten floors and collapsing walls.

His father hadn't been pleased.

Still, Ken gave the building a cursory examination in the hopes of finding a way in.

New boards were secured over the windows on the back side, and Ken sighed.

He kicked a rock, made his way to the wall separating the apartment building from the house next door, and wandered along its edge. The wall came up to his chest, and it was as wide as he was tall. All the stones fit perfectly against one another. There was no mortar holding them together, which, his father had said, was a testament to how they used to build walls.

Ken reached the center of the wall's length when he saw he wasn't alone.

An old man, far older than Mama Cristo, sat in a wooden wheelchair, a quilt wrapped around his shoulders and his gray eyes fixed upon Ken.

Ken's throat tightened, then relaxed. He'd never met the old man before. He had seen him from the safety of his father's pickup, but never in person.

"Good morning, sir," Ken greeted, remembering his manners.

One of the old man's white eyebrows raised up. "Good morning indeed, young sir. Who might you be?"

"I'm Ken," he answered. "Kendall Gunther, sir."

"Well, are you in the Army, perchance, Mr. Gunther?"

Ken blushed. "No, sir. I just like the hat. And the Army."

"Why is that?"

Ken blinked. "My father was in the Army. In Vietnam, sir. My grandfather fought in World War Two."

The old man nodded. "Well then, Mr. Gunther, my name is Mr. Essex. I was in the Army, too, you see."

Ken stepped closer to the wall. "You were?"

"Indeed, I was," Mr. Essex confirmed. "I did not fight in World War Two, though."

"When were you in the Army?"

Mr. Essex smiled. "I was in the Army until nineteen-eighteen."

"That means you were in during World War One." Ken couldn't keep the surprise out of his voice. "I've never met anyone who was in that war before."

"There aren't many of us left, to be perfectly honest." Mr. Essex unlocked the wheels on his chair, maneuvered it so he could face Ken, and then secured his wheels once more. "My brothers fought in the war, too. Except they didn't fight in the American Army."

Ken frowned. "How could they not fight in the US Army?"

"My youngest brother, Oliver, he managed to get across the ocean to England, and he joined the British Army. My older brother, Nathaniel, he went up to Canada and enlisted with the Canadians. I couldn't go with them, you see."

"No, we didn't go until, um, nineteen-seventeen."

"How old are you, Mr. Gunther?"

"I'm eleven, sir."

"I am impressed," Mr. Essex stated. "There are a great many adults who do not know when the US entered the war. Yes, I'm very impressed. How did you learn this? Was it your father?"

Ken shook his head. "No, sir. I read a lot. A real lot. Some of my teachers say I read too much."

Mr. Essex made a sour face. "You can never read too much, Mr. Gunther. Never. Let me assure you of that. Had I not read as much as I did, I never would have passed law school, nor would I have been a successful lawyer." The man motioned towards the large house behind him. "And I would most certainly not have been able to live so comfortably. Regardless, back to the point. I am most impressed with you."

Ken's blush returned. He cleared his throat and then asked, "Do your brothers live nearby?"

Mr. Essex shook his head. "Neither of my brothers survived the war, I'm afraid. They are buried in Europe. Oliver died of his wounds in England, and so he is buried outside of Surrey. As for Nathaniel, his remains were never found."

"I'm sorry," Ken said.

"I am, too, Mr. Gunther," Mr. Essex sighed. "The war took a great deal from me. Both my brothers and my legs."

Ken frowned and looked at Mr. Essex's legs, which were clad in corduroy pants. The old man grinned.

"They look right as rain, don't they?" Mr. Essex asked.

"Yes."

"Even my shoes are polished."

Ken had to agree they were. The black shoes glowed in the sunlight.

Mr. Essex leaned forward, closed both hands into fists, and rapped on his shins. A dull sound rolled out. At Ken's surprised expression, Mr. Essex laughed.

"They are made of wood, Mr. Gunther." The old man returned to his upright position. "I'm certain I could afford something newer, something plastic. I'm wealthy enough, I could probably equip myself as old Ahab did, eh?"

"I don't know who Ahab is," Ken confessed.

"Ah, that is something we will have to rectify then," Mr. Essex smiled. "You stay here, and I will fetch the book for you. It won't take me but a minute or two. The copy is on my desk. I often look at it."

The smile faded from the old man's face. "It was my brother Nathaniel's book. I adored him, you know. I looked up to him. He was everything I wanted to be. And Oliver, well, he was as sweet as a puppy."

Mr. Essex cleared his throat, and he looked at Ken.

"I love America, Mr. Gunther," the old man stated, his voice hoarse. "Fighting for her, for everything she stands for, that was certainly worth both my legs. The war claimed both my brothers, though. Both of them, and I can tell you this, Mr. Gunther, nothing was worth that. Not a single item or idea was worth one of their lives, let alone both."

Mr. Essex took a deep breath and let it out slowly. He wiped his eyes, took a pocket square out of his shirt pocket, and dried his hands.

"Ah, Captain Ahab," Mr. Essex murmured. Looking at Ken, he asked, "Will you wait a moment or two? I know Nathaniel would want you to have the book. It was his favorite."

"Yes," Ken agreed. "I'll wait, Mr. Essex."

The old man smiled, unlocked the wheels of his chair, and rolled himself toward the house. Ken stood at the stonewall, his hands in his pockets, and he waited.

MOBY DICK

Ken sat on the couch, curled up with the book open and resting against his knees. A faint odor of pipe tobacco drifted out as he turned the page, and Ken found himself looking at a picture of Queequeg. The drawing of the harpooneer showed heavy tattoos on the man's face, and Ken stared at it, unable to look away.

The creak of floorboards caught his attention, and he dragged his eyes away to look at his father, who stood in the doorway, a bottle of beer in his hand.

"What're you reading, Kid?"

"*Moby Dick*," Ken answered, closing the book and straightening up.

His father came into the room and sat down in his chair. "That's a good-looking book."

Ken smiled. "Colonel Essex gave it to me."

His father's brow furrowed for a moment and then smoothed with recognition of the name. "Damn. Forgot he was a colonel. He's the crippled guy, right?"

Ken nodded.

"Damned hard, man." Ken's father spoke with admiration. "Lot of guys wouldn't do anything after losing both their legs. Did you know he was a lawyer in town?"

"Yes."

"Good one, too," the man murmured. He finished his beer. "You like the book?"

"Yes."

"Hard to read?"

Ken thought about it and then answered, "A little."

"A little. Good. I read it when I was a little older than you. Melville's great. Wait until you get out on the sea with him. Old Ahab's got a couple of screws loose." His father grunted and chuckled before he let out a belch, then tapped his own head with the empty bottle. The clunk of the thick bottom of the glass filled the room. "Seeing as it's Friday, you can stay up late. I'm waitin' on a few of the guys. You want to hang around or read in the bedroom?"

"I'll hang around." Ken stood up, holding his book. "I just need to put this away."

His father grinned. "Good. You'll be pouring out the punishment, alright?"

Ken giggled. "Yeah. I like to do that."

"I know you do, Kid. Alright, put your book away and keep an ear out for the guys. Some of them might be three sheets to the wind by the time they get here. And don't take any shit from them if they are. They know better. Got it?"

"Got it."

Holding the book to his chest, Ken left the front room for the bedroom he shared with his father, placing his book on the nightstand by his cot. He let his hand linger on the book for a moment, then, with a smile, he made his way to the kitchen to gather up the glasses his father's guests would need for the games.

LEE CAMPBELL

"Come on, Kid, you're killing me," Danny howled as the small room shook with laughter.

Ken grinned and poured the whiskey until it filled the tumbler. He was careful not to spill any of the liquor. The gouged and battered coffee table, maimed by slammed bottles and littered with the ash of cigarettes, cigars and playing cards, stood as the centerpiece of the room. Half a dozen of his father's co-workers occupied kitchen chairs, a box, and the floor while his father sat in his armchair, smiling with benevolence upon all those gathered.

"Those are the rules, Danny," Bucky chuckled. "You lose the hand, you drink a shot."

"That's a pint, not a shot," Danny argued, gesturing to the tumbler full of whiskey. "Kid doesn't know what he's doing."

"Danny," Ken's father silenced the room. Danny shrank a little in his seat. "I told my son how to pour them."

Ken heard the inflection of the words, and so too did the gathered men.

Danny cleared his throat, picked up the tumbler and muttered, "Sorry, Mike. Sorry, Kid."

As the man drank the whiskey, Ken looked at his father.

"Do me a favor, Kid," his father said, "go outside and check the front porch. See if Lee got lost again."

Ken nodded and went to set the bottle of whiskey down when his father stopped him with a shake of the head. "Take it with you. Lee thinks better when he's got some whiskey in him." Mutters of agreement issued from the other men as Ken left the room with the bottle in hand. He followed the well-familiar path of the hallway to the apartment's propped-open door. Traveling down the narrow stairs, he passed the Cristos' open door and remembered all the sights and sounds of when he would see Henri sitting with Grandmother Cristo.

When Ken reached the porch, he turned left, careful to avoid rotten boards and a scattered collection of rusting car parts and piles of broken furniture. Beyond the porch's roof, the stars pulsed in the cool air, and when he rounded the corner to the front of the building, Ken found Lee.

The man sat on the top step of the broad granite stairs, an unlit cigarette in his mouth, his face tilted up at a slight angle and wearing a vacant expression. The stars reflected in his eyes and the same light was absorbed in the dark blue knit cap that was a permanent part of Lee's attire.

Ken cleared his throat, and when the man didn't react, Ken said, "Mr. Campbell?"

The man blinked, turned his head and looked at Ken. He blinked again, and a smile spread across his face.

"Lee, Kid," the man replied, his words exiting his mouth slowly as if each was difficult to pronounce. "My name's Lee. My father is Mr. Campbell, and he's a son of a bitch."

Lee's eyes shifted from Ken's face to the whiskey in his hands, and Ken passed it over to him.

As Lee accepted the bottle, Ken saw the sharp, pale scars that formed an intricate pattern on the back of the man's hand. Lee let out a pleased sigh and removed the bottle's cap. He took a small sip, and Ken saw a brightness appear in Lee's eyes.

Lee took a longer drink, smacked his lips and let out a deep chuckle. "So good, Kid."

Ken smiled.

"Your father worried I got lost?" Lee took another drink, lowering the level of the whiskey in the bottle, his words coming out faster.

"Yes," Ken answered, struggling to stop himself from adding, 'sir.'

"Huh." Lee drank again, the whiskey flowing as easily as water down the man's throat.

Ken stood on the porch, waiting for Lee to get to his feet.

But Lee drank. After several minutes of silence, in which Ken wasn't quite certain if the man knew he was still there, Lee spoke.

"You know, the stars look different in Vietnam, Kid?"

"No," Ken lied. His father had mentioned it in passing. Lee spoke infrequently, though, and Ken wanted to hear what the man had to say.

"Hm." Lee raised the bottle again, and Ken saw it was now two-thirds empty. "They are. I didn't notice until I got hit. Spent a lot of time on my back, staring up. Through the tracers and the haze, I could see the stars. I could see how bright they were."

Lee reached up, took off his hat, and for the first time, Ken saw the man's unadorned scalp. Lee ran his hand over scarred flesh, some of it raised up, others cutting deep grooves into the skin. For the first time, Ken saw Lee was earless. Only holes stood where ears had once been.

Lee drank from the bottle, and without looking at Ken, the man stated, "You've never seen my scars."

"No," Ken agreed.

"I don't take my hat off too often," Lee continued, and Ken wasn't sure if the man had heard his response.

"I used to," Lee said after a pause to take a small sip of whiskey. "When I first got home and out of Walter Reed down in Maryland. I used to take my hat on and off. Just like everybody else. Thing is, Kid, I'm not."

Lee stopped, and Ken expected the man to lapse back into his old, familiar silence.

Lee didn't.

"It took me a while to understand what was going on," Lee added. "My brains, they got a little scrambled from the concussion. Most people thought I was deformed or I'd been injured at work or in an accident. When I told them I was wounded in Vietnam, stuff got funny."

Lee paused and took a long drink,

"Lot of stupid shit about Vietnam, Kid," Lee continued. "Protesting. Your Dad knows. Won't talk about it. You know he couldn't get a job when he got back from 'Nam?"

Ken shook his head.

"It's true," Lee nodded. "People would ask him what he did, and your dad, well, he's your Dad. He told them. Finally, after the third interview, your Dad asked why he wasn't qualified. Guy told your dad he was, just wasn't hiring a killer. You believe that bullshit?"

Ken remained silent as Lee looked at the nearly empty bottle.

"It was different for me," Lee sighed, running his free hand over his scarred scalp. "People felt bad for me. Asked what happened. Your Dad ever tell you?"

Ken shook his head. "I asked once, and he said I should ask you."

Lee chuckled. "Sounds about right for your dad. The official story is I jumped on a grenade to save my lieutenant."

Ken waited as Lee finished the whiskey.

"But it's not what happened, Ken." Lee put the cap back on the bottle and set it down on the porch beside him. "See, first of all, it wasn't a grenade. Grenade is the real deal. Solid infantry weapon. Thing is, we were squared off against Victor Charlie, where I was stationed. Whole lot of rice paddies with homemade long guns for hunting monkeys and Molotov cocktails. You know what that is?"

"No," Ken admitted. "I've heard of it, but I don't know what it is."

"Molotov cocktail's a homemade explosive. Gasoline, oil, a bottle, a rag, and a match," Lee explained. "Nothin' to it."

Ken edged closer.

Lee lifted his free hand to his scalp, tracing the scars.

"Well," the man continued, returning his hand to his lap. "Old Victor Charlie sent a Molotov over, and damned if it didn't get up close and personal with my lieutenant's gear. He had his webbing off, a frag and some mags laid out, and when that Molotov landed, the lieutenant shoved me onto it."

Lee looked at the empty whiskey bottle.

"They don't tell you that part," the man chuckled. "They don't. Makes you wonder how many guys were decorated for 'selflessly' jumping on a grenade. How many were pushed?"

Lee held the empty bottle out, and Ken took it from him. Lee put on his hat before he stood up, weaving from left to right and then back again as he often did, with or without whiskey in him.

Putting his scarred hand on Ken's shoulder, Lee smiled. "Take point, little man, else I'm liable to fall asleep out here."

Ken nodded and proudly "took point" as his father and the man's friends called it, guiding the wounded man through the wreckage on the porch.

GOING TO THE BASE

Ken stood in the kitchen and looked outside. Heavy snow had fallen across Norwich the night before, blowing in off the Atlantic and adding several more inches to the snow that had been piling up for the previous three weeks.

He shivered at the sight of it and once more wished he could stay home.

"You 'bout ready, Kid?" his father asked from the hallway.

"Yes," Ken answered. He picked up his backpack and opened it. Ken saw the minibox of Fruit Loops his father had given him, as well as a box of Good & Plenty candy. There was a bottle of Very Fine Fruit Punch too. Beside it, wrapped in an old tee shirt to keep it safe, was his newest book, *Typhoon of Steel*. His father had found it for him at the used bookstore downtown.

Ken had finished *Moby Dick* a few days earlier, and he still had to speak with Colonel Essex about it.

Ken wanted to know more about the Colonel's brother, Nathaniel. What had made *Moby Dick* so special to him? Were there other books of Nathaniel's that the Colonel had kept?

His father came into the kitchen, poured out the last little bit from his coffee mug and rinsed it before setting it beside the small sink.

"You got your food packed?" his father asked.

Ken nodded.

"And you brought a book to read?"

"Yes. The new one."

His father smiled. "Good. Now, I'm not sure how long this meeting is going to last. I didn't even know the Commander was going to call it until this morning. The sub base has been crazy since word came down about an issue with one of the Trident's batteries. Word has it that the Navy's sending in investigators down to Lower Base to make sure that all the used materials we're shipping out are going where they're supposed to."

Ken's father shook his head. "Navy's crazy, Kid. Glad I'm a civilian, that's for damned sure. But that's beside the point. Listen, you need to make sure you eat, and if you need anything, you can speak with the Commander's assistant. Got it?"

"Got it."

"You're not close to being done with the book, right?"

Ken thought about it and then shook his head. "No. There's a lot left. I won't finish it today."

"Okay." His father tugged at his mustache. "Yeah, that's it. Take point, Kid. Who knows, maybe I'll even let you drive the truck."

Ken giggled as he picked up his bag. "I can't reach the pedals."

"I'll put blocks on your feet," his father answered, laughing. "Alright, enough BS. Let's go. Move it out, Kid."

With his father behind him and the weight of the backpack on his shoulder, Ken led the way out of their small apartment.

SERGEANT JOHN HUTCHINS

Outside, the wind ripped up off the Atlantic and rattled the tall windows in their casings. The dull white blinds hissed as they rubbed against one another.

Ken sat in a hard plastic chair, reading *Typhoon of Steel*, which was about the battle for Okinawa in World War Two. The dustjacket was rubbed raw in some places and dirty in others, and the book smelled faintly of cigarettes. On the inside cover was a book-plate of what his father had called a family crest. The name 'White' occupied the center of the crest, and Ken wondered if the previous owner of the book had smoked.

Ken shifted himself in the seat, angling the book to catch the afternoon light on the old, thick pages. It wasn't often he had to accompany his father to work, but since they had canceled school because of snow, his father had to bring him in. Mama Cristo had a cold, and she couldn't watch him.

So, instead of sitting with Mama Cristo listening to Haitian music and drinking tea, Ken was waiting for his father, who was in the Commander's office of the Groton Submarine Base, for an unscheduled meeting.

As he read, Ken occasionally glanced up at the Commander's assistant. The man wore a starched khaki uniform and worked on a new computer, the keys of the keyboard clicking and clacking beneath the man's rapidly moving fingers. In another plastic chair to the left of the Commander's door sat an old man. The man's civilian clothes were neatly pressed, his shoes shined, and his white hair clipped close to the skin. The old man peered at Ken over the top of a magazine called *Leatherneck*.

After a moment, the old man closed the magazine and put it down on the small table beside his chair.

"What are you reading, son?" the old man asked.

"*Typhoon of Steel*, sir," Ken answered, politely closing the book.

"How old are you?"

"Eleven, sir," Ken replied.

"And you're Mike's boy?" the man inquired.

"Yes, sir."

"Of course you are," the old man smiled. "You read a lot?"

"Yes, sir."

"Good."

The old man took a pack of cigarettes and a lighter out of his breast pocket, put a cigarette in his mouth, lit it, then put the pack and the lighter away. He exhaled and looked at Ken through the smoke. "You know why I smoke, son?"

Ken shook his head.

"Because of those damned islands, including Okinawa."

Ken felt his eyes widen. "You were there?"

The old man nodded. "I carried a flame thrower. Had to corkscrew and blowtorch those little sl—"

The assistant looked up from his computer. "John."

"Ah hell," the old man snapped. "What in the hell am I supposed to call those bastards, Eddie? Imperial Japanese soldiers?"

John grumbled, stabbing the cigarette at the assistant. "Fuck that. Besides, he's Mike's boy. I'm sure he's heard worse."

Ken couldn't say no. He had heard worse, much worse, from his father.

The assistant sighed, shook his head, and returned to his work.

"Anyway," John continued, turning his attention back to Ken. "When I was on Okinawa, I carried the flame thrower. God damned heavy weapon. I was only a hundred pounds in my boondockers, and when that pig was full, she weighed right around seventy pounds. Big old bomb strapped on my back.

"Lost a few friends to those blowing up," the old man mused. He looked at his cigarette. "You know what, though?"

"No sir, what?" Ken asked.

"It was worth the risk. Those fuckin'," he caught himself. "Those sons-of-bitches were terrified of that God damned thing. You could hear 'em hollering in their holes and their boxes when they knew I was coming."

The old man leaned forward.

"You see, we worked in teams. Did you know that?"

Ken shook his head.

"Well, we did," John said. "Couple of riflemen and a BAR man, you know what a BAR man was?"

"Yes sir," Ken answered. "Browning automatic rifle."

"Good boy!" John grinned. "You're just as smart as father said you are. Anyway, where was I? Oh yeah, the BAR man and a couple of riflemen would put down some suppressing fire on the Jap position, and then another guy with a satchel charge or grenades would work his way up and toss the explosives into the gun port. Now," the old man said, his voice dropping low, "when that happened, I'd follow right behind them and cook those little bastards."

The old man nodded to himself and settled into his chair once more. "See, my kid brother was killed at Tarawa. And every Japanese soldier, sailor, man, wo-man, child, whatever, they needed to pay. And that's where the flame thrower came in.

"Most guys thought I was nuts, but I knew how afraid the Japs were of it. And I hope that they felt the same kind of fear my brother felt wading through that fucking water into machine-gun fire.

"Christ," the old man swore, mashing the butt of his cigarette out in the ashtray beside him. "I must've fried hundreds of the bastards. Maybe a thousand. Maybe more."

"Really?" Ken asked. A mingled sense of fascination and horror whirled within him.

"Really," John grunted as he lit another cigarette. "Anyway, where the hell was I?"

"The cigarettes, sir. Why do you smoke them," Ken reminded him.

John smiled. "That's right. You're bright and polite. Speaks well about your father, son."

"Thank you, sir."

John waved the thanks away, took a pull off the cigarette, then he held it in front of him, looking at the glowing tip and the smoke curling up from it.

"I started smoking these 'cause of the smell of death. Not the ones I cooked, but the others." He put the cigarette back into his mouth. "Well, those others, Son, they got up to a hell of a stink."

"John," the assistant cautioned.

Both Ken and John looked over at the Commander's assistant.

"Maybe you shouldn't say anymore?" the man advised.

John narrowed his eyes and stabbed the cigarette at the man. "Mind your business, you fucking squid. I don't remember asking you for your goddamned opinion. He's a smart boy."

The assistant raised an eyebrow and shook his head.

"Ah, what the fuck do you know," John grunted, looking back to Ken. "He's just pissy 'cause I won't tell him anything and the Commander pulled him off driving duty. That's my job, now. Commander likes having a combat vet drive for him. Plus, I've known the Commander since he was in his momma's belly. His dad and I served together on Okinawa after the war. Kept those fuckin' Japanese, that better Eddie, *Japanese*, in line.

"Your father, Son, he knows the deal. He's been in it." The old man finished the cigarette, grinding the butt out in the tray. "But yeah, picked up the habit because of those damned *Japanese*. The stench was godawful. Bodies just rotting in the Pacific heat. Ain't nothin' like it. Nothin' at all. Besides, the cigarettes help calm my nerves, too. I don't sleep much, Son, not much at all."

The old man looked down at his fingers, and Ken saw the way they trembled.

Ken remained silent, the sound of the assistant typing filling the room.

"I remember things now," John sighed. "I do. Things that I'd thought I'd forgotten. Terrible things."

John lit another cigarette, looking up at the ceiling as he exhaled. "At Peleliu, they cut us apart as we landed. I saw Tommy get cut in half by a Nambu, and I swear some of the Skipper's brains ended up in my mouth.

"Getting off of that beach and into the coral was hard as hell, son," John muttered, looking at Ken. "Your friends get hurt, and you want to help them. But you can't. You have to leave them, you got to go forward. And as you go forward, and everyone's dying or getting hit, and they're screaming and begging for help, it's so loud. Everything's so damned loud. You get scared. Terribly scared. You just want to hide, but you don't.

"No," John said, shaking his head. "You're a Marine, by God. You're a goddamned Marine. You do what you're taught to. Get off the fucking beach and bring the fight to the fucking enemy.

"Peleliu is where I first smoked," John confided. "There were so many dead that they couldn't be buried right away.

"The heat on that damned island," the old Marine muttered.

"Hard work," he continued, "lugging that bitch into position. Cooking them in their holes."

Ken held the book tightly, listening. He watched John smoke his cigarette, the man's eyes half-closed.

The assistant cleared his throat, and John and Ken looked over at him.

"Did they stink as they burned?" the assistant asked.

"The *Japanese?*" Scorned filled John's voice..

The assistant nodded.

Ken looked back to John, and a faraway smile crept onto the old man's face.

"No," John murmured. "Not at all. They kind of smelled like a pig roast. Just made me hungry."

The assistant settled into his chair, an expression of horror on his face, and Ken found himself wondering how a burning person could smell like roasting pig.

HOMEWORK

"Mr. Gunther!"

Ken paused as he walked up the driveway and saw Colonel Essex sitting in his wheelchair on his porch. The man waved and Ken waved in reply. He walked to the wall and brushed some of the snow off the stones.

"Returning from school, young Master Gunther?" Colonel Essex inquired.

"Yes sir," Ken answered.

"And did we learn anything of interest today?"

Ken frowned. "I don't think so. We talked a little about the French and Indian War."

"Ah, an interesting bit of American history," the man stated, nodding. "Did you know, your home was once owned by a man whose family could be traced back to the first of the settlers in this area?"

Ken shook his head. "No sir, I didn't."

"It's true." Colonel Essex paused. "Mrs. Dunne, my part-time housekeeper is here. Would you care for a bit of tea and perhaps a cookie or two?"

Ken's stomach grumbled at the thought of a cookie and he nodded. "Yes please."

"Excellent," Colonel Essex said.

Ken started back towards the street when the man called out to him again. Looking over his shoulder, Ken saw Colonel Essex shake his head.

"No, no, Mr. Gunther," the Colonel smiled. "You are a boy, travel as boys are wont to do. Up and over the wall with you, sir, if you are so inclined."

Ken giggled, climbed up onto the snow covered stonewall and dropped into Colonel Essex's yard. He brushed the snow from his pants and coat, and then hurried along the man's freshly plowed driveway to the front steps. As he climbed up them, a woman who was younger than Colonel Essex but older than his father opened the door.

"Who is this, Colonel?" she asked.

"This, Mrs. Dunne, is my neighbor, Mr. Kendall Gunther. I have invited him in for tea and cookies," Colonel Essex explained.

"Come right in, then, gentlemen," Mrs. Dunne smiled, holding the door open.

Ken followed Colonel Essex into the house and paused in a small room to kick the snow off his boots. As Colonel Essex rolled through another doorway, Mrs. Dunne held out her hands.

"You can leave your coat and such with me, Kendall," she said, her voice gentle. "Never mind about the boots. You can keep them on. I need to mop the floors later anyway."

Ken nodded shyly, took off his backpack and handed her his coat, hat and gloves.

"Mr. Gunther," Colonel Essex asked from the hallway. "Do you have homework?"

"Yes sir," Ken answered. "Some spelling words and a worksheet for science."

"Difficult?"

Ken shook his head.

"Then leave your rucksack with Mrs. Dunne as well," Colonel Essex stated. "We shan't have anything interrupt your impromptu history lesson."

Mrs. Dunne hung up Ken's belongings in a small closet and asked Colonel Essex, "Do you want to take your tea in the library, Colonel?"

"Yes, please," he replied.

"Just follow the Colonel, Kendall," she stated. "I'll be along shortly with tea and cookies."

"Okay. And you can just call me Ken," he smiled.

"Ken," she said with a wink. She gave him a soft pat on the cheek and then ushered him toward Colonel Essex.

"This way, Mr. Gunther," he said. "This way."

Ken followed the man down the hallway and then left into a large room lined with shelves of books and curious mementos. A huge desk of dark wood occupied a position near a pair of windows that looked out toward Washington Street and a comfortable looking chair sitting off to the right of a fireplace. The familiar rumbling hiss of steam rattled through a nearby radiator, and Ken looked in awe at the books lining the shelves.

"You will be free to peruse those at your leisure, young Master Gunther," Colonel Essex informed him. "First though, take a seat and get yourself comfortable. Is it too warm in here for you?"

"No sir," Ken assured him. "I like it. A lot."

Colonel Essex smiled. "Good."

As Ken sat down, the Colonel parked his wheelchair on the opposite side of a small tea table set close to Ken's chair.

Mrs. Dunne entered a moment later with a silver tray. Upon it stood two porcelain teacups, a matching plate loaded with chocolate chip cookies, and small containers of cream and sugar. The teapot, which matched the rest of the set, had steam rising from its curled spout.

"Thank you, Mrs. Dunne," Colonel Essex said, and Ken added his own thank you as well.

The woman set the tray on the table, smiled and left the room.

"Do you take cream and sugar?" Colonel Essex asked.

"Yes sir," Ken answered, eyeing the cookies.

"Take a cookie, Mr. Gunther," Colonel Essex smiled. "We are not standing on ceremony here."

"Thank you." Ken picked up a warm cookie and bit into it. He chewed and watched as the Colonel dropped two cubes of sugar into a cup, added a little cream, and then poured the tea.

"I always find it easier to pour the tea last," Colonel Essex explained. "The sound of a spoon against china is tiresome to me."

Colonel Essex placed the teacup in front of Ken.

"Now, Mr. Gunther, your home. I take it there are more than two apartments in there?" Colonel Essex asked.

Ken nodded, finished chewing and said, "Yes sir. There's ours, the Cristos', Antonio's, Sylvia's, and the Santiagos. They live on the first floor. The Christos live in the middle and we live on part of the third floor. Antonio and Sylvia, they each have an apartment on the other side of us. My dad and I usually can't hear them, though. My dad says they work third shift so they're usually not around when we are."

"You've been there for some time, haven't you?"

"Yes sir," Ken answered. "I think about ten years. That's what my dad said."

"You know," the Colonel began. "I never paid much attention to the building. Not after John Coffin died in 1962. His oldest boy, Caleb, he is the one who turned it into apartments. A shame, really. It was a beautiful home."

Colonel Essex smiled. "My apologies, Mr. Gunther. I am sure it is a beautiful home still."

"You don't have to apologize," Ken said. He looked at the cookies again.

"Help yourself."

Ken smiled and took another cookie.

"You know, I have spoken to your father before," Colonel Essex stated.

"I know, sir," Ken smiled. "He mentioned it the other night after you gave me *Moby Dick*."

"Did you enjoy it?" Colonel Essex asked, all thoughts about the house forgotten.

Ken nodded his head happily. "It was great. Captain Ahab really had some problems."

Colonel Essex laughed and clapped his hands. "Yes, yes he did, Mr. Gunther. I am so glad you liked it."

"I wanted to ask, are there any other books you think I might like?"

"Oh, there are indeed," Colonel Essex answered with a grin. "We shall discuss that after our cookies and tea. I do have one more question, if you don't mind my asking, Mr. Gunther."

Ken shook his head and chewed the last bit of the second cookie.

"Your father, he works for the Navy, does he not?"

"He does," Ken said. "He works on lower base in Groton. He gets rid of stuff for the Navy."

"A decent paying job," Colonel Essex murmured. Then, a little louder he added, "Does your father ever talk about moving?"

"No. Sometimes, his friends ask him why he doesn't move," Ken answered. "He tells them he likes it. Good neighbors and he can put money away."

"For retirement?"

"No sir," Ken said. "He says he wants me to go to a good college and get a good job. He told them he can't do that if he's worried about a mortgage."

"Do you ever want to move?" Colonel Essex asked.

Ken shook his head. "I like it here. Plus, we just met, Colonel Essex. I like to talk to you."

The older man smiled. "The feeling is quite mutual, I assure you, Mr. Gunther. Now, you were asking about book recommendations?"

"Yes," Ken confirmed. He took a sip of the tea and shivered with delight.

Colonel Essex's smile broadened. "Very good. My brother, Nathaniel, he was exceptionally fond of seafaring tales. Have you ever heard of *Captains Courageous* by Rudyard Kipling?"

"No sir."

"We shall have to rectify that, then, Mr. Gunther," Colonel Essex declared, taking a sip of his own tea. "I shall fetch it for you soon. Tell me, do you like the cookies?"

Grinning, Ken picked up another cookie. "Yes sir."

He popped it into his mouth and Colonel Essex let out a loud, pleased laugh.

CROSSING THE YARD

Ken clutched his book to his chest beneath the protection of his winter coat. Snow fell in heavy flakes to the battered pavement of the lower sub base in New London, Connecticut, and Ken hurried alongside his father. While Ken wore a knitted cap, courtesy of Mrs. Cristo, his father didn't.

His father had turned the collar up on his coat to keep the snow from falling down his neck, his long black hair hidden, and the man's head moved back and forth. His father's eyes seemed to miss nothing as he looked from left to right, and there was a smooth, dangerous way in which he moved across the ground. Ken could see parts of himself in his father. Not the graceful movements or the steady eye, but the dark hair and the high forehead. Mrs. Cristo had pointed it out to him, and it brought a question to Ken's mind.

For a moment, he held onto it, glanced at his father's face in the falling snow and then judged it safe to ask.

"Hey, Dad."

His father looked down at him, brow furrowed. "What's up, Kid?"

"Um, can I ask a question?"

His father slowed his pace. "Sure."

"Do I look like my mom?"

Ken's father came to a stop, and Ken did as well. Fear welled up within him, and he tightened his grip on the book. He braced himself for his father's anger, to hear the rage the man kept on a short leash.

That anger flickered across the man's face, but it vanished as did the furrows in his brow.

"Yeah," his father nodded. "A bit. You've got her eyes, Kid. Same blue-green. You kind of move like her, too. Like you know that you're never going to fall."

His father pulled at his mustache. "It's hard, sometimes, to notice her in you."

Ken frowned. "Why?"

His father let out a soft, bitter chuckle. "Believe it or not, Ken, I loved your mom. With all my heart. She just didn't love us the same way. That's a damned hard thing. I mean, yeah, it was a slap to your old man's ego, but it was worse than that."

Ken waited as his father took a deep breath.

"See, it's not often a woman takes off without the kid," his father continued. "There's a thing called the maternal instinct. I don't know what happened to your mom's. Either she wasn't born with it or, well, having a good time was just that much more important."

Ken's next question surprised himself, and he whispered, "Was she nice to me?"

Ken's father shook his head. "No. Not really. I used to come home on my lunch break to make sure your diaper was changed, and you got your food. Sometimes, your Aunt Mary would come over to help. She was really good, used to lay into your mother something fierce. But they were sisters, and your mom never seemed to care what Mary said to her. Mary even hung around a bit after your mom took off, but then she got a decent job out in Chicago and had to move."

His father wiped a bit of snow off his own forehead. "What made you think of that, Kid?"

"I was watching you look around and walk," Ken answered. "I know I don't move like you, so I was wondering if I moved like her."

His father smiled and shook his head. "You're a bright kid, Ken. I move the way I do because of Vietnam. Something you pick up, if you're around a place like that long enough. You get, I don't know. Jumpy. You look around to make sure everything is okay. Two years in country will do that to you. If you moved like that, Kid, well, I'd be a little worried."

His father paused, seemed to consider something, and then shrugged. "Come on, let's get over to the cafeteria. This snow is driving me crazy, and I bet you want to read."

Ken nodded and hurried after his father, the snow falling heavier and thoughts of his mother fading in the cold air.

CORPORAL BILL RICHARDSON

Ken and his father entered the cafeteria near his father's building on the lower portion of the Groton Submarine Base.

As they walked through the large room, Ken's father guided him towards a long table set at the back of the cafeteria. A pair of men, slightly younger than Ken's father, sat at the table.

His father frowned at them.

"Got to get up, guys," his father ordered, stopping a few feet away from the table. "Combat vets only."

"Seriously, Mike?" one of them asked.

"Does it look like I'm joking?" Ken's father snapped. "This table was only for combat vets before I started here. So, get the fuck up and get the fuck out,"

Ken's father snarled, jerking the thumb of his free hand over his shoulder.

The two men grumbled, cast nervous glances at Ken's father, and then picked up their trays as they stood. His father's expression remained unyielding until the men had retreated to a table far across the room.

His father shook his head as he helped Ken pull a chair over to the table

"They're morons," his father explained, putting his coffee down. "You sure you don't want anything?"

Ken nodded. His stomach was still full of the scrambled eggs and toast they'd had for breakfast.

His father shrugged. "You'll need to eat a big dinner tonight, okay?"

Again, Ken nodded.

"Gotta try and put some weight on you before football starts up again. No more tucking weights into your pants to make weigh-in. Ah hell," Ken's father broke off, grinning, "there's Bill."

Ken turned in his seat and saw a man older than his dad walk into the cafeteria. The man's thick wrists protruded from the frayed ends of his gray sweater, and he shuffled as he walked. His faded black slacks whispered against one another as though telling a story no one else should hear. Ken couldn't tell if the man's stiff posture came from the way he walked or if the way he walked caused it. Bill reached up and ran a hand through his wild, silver hair as a pair of reading glasses bounced across his broad chest, suspended by a golden chain.

Bill lowered his hand and rubbed at his chin with slow, methodical movements. The man glanced around the room, but Ken knew he wasn't seeing anything.

Sometimes, when he couldn't sleep, Ken had seen the same look late at night on his father's face.

"Bill," Ken's father called out, concern heavy in his voice.

The older man stood still, his hands dropping down to his sides, where they opened and closed with a staccato rhythm.

"Bill," Ken's father pitched his voice a little deeper and sent the name rolling across the cafeteria's lino-leum floor. Others turned their heads to look, but Bill remained where he stood, ignorant of Ken's father.

Ken heard his father inhale just as Bill turned to face them. A smile, absent of most of its teeth, appeared on Bill's face, and the man started towards them, moving with his stiff, awkward march across the cafeteria.

"Saw a couple of shitbirds at our table earlier, Mike," Bill stated as he reached them. He paused, adjusted his belt, grunted, pulled out a chair and sat down heavily in it.

He looked at Ken's father, nodded, and then he turned his attention to Ken. Bill winked at him. "Don't realize how important toes are until they're gone, Kid."

"Toes?" Ken asked, making sure he had heard Bill correctly.

"Toes," Bill answered.

"Bill fought in Korea, Ken," Ken's father informed him. "You know when Korea was?"

Ken nodded. "Between World War Two and Vietnam."

"Good job, Kid," his father grinned.

Ken's cheeks grew hot, and Bill grunted in approval.

"Nicely done, Ken," Bill said. "Most people don't even know there was a Korean War. Fucking Truman. Called the whole thing a police action so he wouldn't piss off the Commies. Fuck them. Oh shit."

"What?" Ken's father asked.

"Forgot my coffee," Bill sighed.

"I'll get it," Ken's father offered. "Want anything else?"

"Blueberry muffin," Bill replied. He pulled a five-dollar bill out of his wallet and passed it to Ken's dad. Looking over at Ken, Bill asked, "You like chocolate milk?"

"Yes, sir," Ken said.

"Get the boy a chocolate milk on me, Mike," Bill told him.

Ken's father gave a curt nod and headed off toward the kitchen and the register.

"Your dad says you like to read, Ken," Bill said.

Ken nodded. "Yes, sir."

"Military history?" Bill asked.

"Yes, sir."

"Have you read about Korea?" Bill asked softly.

"Only a little," Ken answered.

Bill nodded. "Ever seen the name Chosin in your readings?"

Ken shook his head.

"Coldest place on Earth, far as I'm concerned." A small, humorless smile stole onto Bill's face. "Terrible cold, Son. Settles into your bones for-goddamn-ever. You're never warm because you never forget that cold. No. Not Chosin's cold." Bill rubbed his hands, his gaze slipping away for a heartbeat. "You know what we call ourselves?"

"No, sir," Ken answered.

"The Chosin Frozen," Bill told him. "When we were up around that fucking reservoir, you'd drop your pants, shit, and before that turd had time to hit the snow, well, it was already frozen."

"Talking about Chosin?" Ken's father asked as he sat down at the table with a plastic tray. From it he removed Bill's order, putting the older man's coffee and blueberry muffin near Bill and a bottle of chocolate milk in front of Ken.

"Thanks, Dad," Ken said, twisting the cap off. "Thank you, Sir."

"Name's Bill, son," Bill remarked.

"Okay, Bill," Ken grinned.

"And yes, Mike, talking about Chosin," Bill nodded.

"Figured," Ken's father smiled. He opened a wax paper bag and pulled out a pair of plain donuts and dipped one into his own cup of coffee before taking a bite.

He reached for the coffee cup with his right hand, and it took a moment for Ken to realize the last two fingers were missing. Scarred skin stretched over where the digits had once been.

Bill laughed as he picked up the cup. "Noticed those, huh, Kid?"

Ken nodded.

"Frostbite," Bill remarked. He held his hand up and turned it from left to right, allowing Ken to see all sides of it. "That's what happens when you take too long clearing a jam in your rifle at Chosin. Lost all of my toes, too," Bill continued. "All ten of those little piggies turned black and had to be taken off."

"Don't show him your feet, Bill," Ken's father stated, taking a drink of his own coffee.

Bill frowned but shrugged. "Anyway, Kid, take it from me, it's not a pretty sight. Kind of just looks like I'm wearing meat socks. 'Bout as useful, too."

Ken drank his chocolate milk, and silence fell over the table. Ken's father watched Bill, Ken watched his father, and Bill seemed to look through the concrete of the cafeteria.

"It was so cold there," Bill murmured, his eyes fixed on the wall. "I never knew a cold like that. Didn't think it was possible. Couldn't even imagine it. Not like that."

Ken looked to his father, who shook his head and raised a finger to his lips.

"Our weapons didn't fire right," Bill continued, "and the bodies got stiff so quick. Just blocks of meat, frozen like broken toys. When we dragged our dead back, we tried to straighten 'em out so we could load 'em up."

Bill sipped at his coffee. "And those fucking Chinese were everywhere. Tens of thousands of them. They'd blow those damned horns before they'd attack. Sometimes you couldn't see them, but you could always hear them. Thousands of feet on the snow. So many of those bastards didn't have shoes. Some had canvas sneakers, others had boots. But most of them we fought, they were just barefoot. Don't know how in the hell they could march like that."

Bill frowned. The old man twisted in his seat, nose wrinkling.

"What is it?" Ken's father asked, looking around.

"Some asshole's eating garlic," Bill spat. He looked at Ken. "You like garlic?"

Ken shook his head.

"Course not," Bill grunted. He set down his coffee and massaged the stumps of his fingers. "You're a good boy."

Absently, Bill glanced down into his coffee cup. "I hate the smell of garlic. Scares the shit out of me to this day. All those dirty bastards ate was garlic. They smelled like garlic. Just fucking garlic. When the wind shifted, Son, it would carry that stench right to you."

Bill stopped talking, finished his coffee, blinked, smiled and said, "I'm sorry, Mike. What were we talking about?"

"Football," Ken's father answered. "Just trying to figure out if the Patriots have a chance this season."

"Probably not," Bill replied. He broke off a bit of his muffin, popped it into his mouth and added, "Not unless they figure out their passing game."

The conversation drifted back to football, and Ken drank his chocolate milk. His eyes roamed the cafeteria, looking for whoever was eating garlic and reminding Bill of Chosin.

RAIN

The freezing rain hammered the window and shook the side of the house.

Ken lay in his cot, half-listening to the rain until his father cursed in his sleep.

Turning onto his side, Ken looked across the small room at his father, the man's shape distorted by the blanket and sheet covering him. The rain lashed the window again, and his father snarled.

Ken didn't need to look at the clock to know what time it was.

Every night, at 2:30 am, his father woke up.

Ken kept his eyes half-closed and waited.

"Fucking Christ, where's my rifle?"

The wooden slats of his father's bed creaked, and the covers were thrown to the floor as Ken's father sat up. In the dim light cast into the room from the nightlight in the hall, Ken saw the sweat on his father's chest, the man's hair in disarray, and the old scars vivid on his flesh.

"It was right the fuck here," his father grumbled, running his fingers through his hair, his eyes open but not seeing. Then, he straightened up and understanding entered his eyes. His father shook off the last bit of the nightmare clinging to him, looked around and sighed. The man's shoulders sagged, and the slats groaned as Ken's father got to his feet.

Through his half-closed eyes, Ken watched as his father eased open the closet door of their shared bedroom. His father reached up and then took down a cigar box. With the box in hand, his father left the room, and Ken closed his eyes and listened for the familiar sounds. When he was younger, Ken had snuck down the hall to watch his father, to see what he was doing, what secret thing his father did in the middle of the night.

Once, his father had caught him and sent him back to bed. His father had been angry, furious that Ken had spied on him.

Now, Ken listened and waited. He knew what action accompanied every sound.

The light clicked in the kitchen, and there was a soft clunk as the cigar box was placed on the counter. A moment later, Ken heard paper rustling, and he could picture the orange box labeled 'Zigzag' that the paper came from.

He had seen his father perform the routine a thousand times. The small leaves would come out of a plastic bag, and his father would sprinkle them in the center of the paper. His father's hands would be steady and sure, rolling the paper into the semblance of a cigarette, and then, with a small lick, he would press the paper together.

Ken knew the routine, and he waited for the click of the lighter.

It followed a moment later, as did a deep inhalation. There was a pause, and then his father sighed as he exhaled. The sweet and sickening smell of his father's cigarette drifted into the bedroom, and Ken sighed as well.

His father would be back in the bedroom soon, and Ken might or might not be awake to hear it. But his father would return, the cigarette finished and able to sleep.

There would be no more worries that he had lost his rifle.

BOOKS AND REPORT CARD

Ken hadn't looked at his report card.

He knew better than to do that. His father had reprimanded him once, when Ken was in the first grade, about looking at something not addressed to him.

"You see that?" his father had asked. "Says Michael Gunther. Not Kendall Gunther. Michael. It's addressed to me, Kid. You don't open something not addressed to you, got it?"

Ken had got it.

Had never forgotten it.

He finished his bowl of chips, brought it into the kitchen and washed and dried it. The hands on the stove's small clock showed it was 4:55. His father would be home in half an hour, or he would call in the next five minutes.

Ken's eyes shifted from the off-yellow phone hanging on the wall by the fridge to the manilla envelope with his report card on the kitchen table. Ken walked past the table, went to the fridge and took out a bottle of birch beer and poured himself a glass. He carried it out to the front room, sat down and picked up his book.

He couldn't watch any tv until his father came home.

Not even if his homework was done, which it was.

Ken turned to his book mark and was about to read when the phone rang. Still holding the book, he hurried into the kitchen and had the phone out of its cradle by the third ring.

"Hello," Ken answered.

"Hey, Kid," his father greeted. "How're you doin'?"

"Okay. I got my report card today."

"Good or bad?" his father asked, voice casual.

Ken grinned. "I didn't look."

His father laughed. "Good boy. Do me a favor, grab it and read it to me. I won't be home until later. Probably not until after bedtime."

"Um, okay." Ken walked to the table and picked up the report card, the cord of the phone stretched out behind him. He held the handset between his shoulder and his ear, set his book on the table and picked up the report card. He had it out of the folder in a moment and read his grades to his father.

"Math is a B. Science is a B. English is an A. Social Studies is an A. Art and gym are both As. Music is a B minus."

"Those are all good, Kid, except the Music," his father said. "What's going on with that?"

"I don't get it," Ken mumbled. "Ms. Walters says I'm tone deaf."

"Fuck her," his father sighed. "Okay. Those are good though. What did I say, twenty-five cents for every A?"

"No!" Ken laughed. "You said ten dollars for every A and five for every B. Nothing for Cs because Cs are average and we're not."

"You got it, Kid. Looks like I owe you fifty-five dollars. You want to hit the bookstores this weekend?"

"Yes!" Ken twisted around and wrapped himself in the cord, laughing.

"Me too," his father chuckled. "Listen, I already talked to the Cristos. You're going to eat dinner with them, okay?"

"Yes."

"Good boy. I'm proud of you. Keep working hard. Now, go have dinner. I'll see you tonight. Love you, Kid."

"Love you too, Dad."

They said goodbye and Ken unraveled himself from the cord, hanging the phone back up with a happy clack. Humming, he took his book back into the front room. The Christos wouldn't eat until six, so there was plenty of time to read before he went to visit.

Settling into his father's chair, Ken thought of the books he would buy on the weekend.

HENRI'S GRAVE

Ken wandered along Washington Street toward Backus Hospital. His breath rushed out in great clouds from his mouth, and he buried his mittened hands deeper into his coat pockets. It was colder than he had expected, but he had dressed warmly. Yantic Cemetery near the hospital wasn't too far from where he lived, but it was far enough to be a cold walk.

Ken didn't mind the walk, though.

It reminded him of Henri when they used to walk all around the city together.

The memory caused Ken's eyes to tear up, and he paused long enough to brush the tears aside. His father didn't like it when he cried.

A short distance later, Ken turned left onto Williams Street and followed it down to Lafayette Street and Yantic Cemetery. Ken crossed the road, went to the cemetery's entrance and walked in. Off to the right, he saw the long, parked cars of a funeral. A black hearse stood at the front of the line, and as Ken turned off toward the pauper's section, he saw car doors opening.

The sight of them reminded him of Henri's funeral.

His friend had been brought in a hearse, but there had only been a few cars and his father's pickup. Henri hadn't been popular at school, and while their teacher and principal came, no one else had. The Cristos had been refugees and Henri spoke with an accent and a lisp. He had been smaller and thinner than their classmates, and he had often smelled of the strong spices Mama Cristo used to cook with.

Their classmates had made fun of Henri, and of Ken for being his friend.

Ken had been the only child at the funeral.

Ken walked along the cemetery road to the pauper's section and then looked for the twisted tree. The tree was how he found Henri's grave. There was no marker. The Cristos hadn't been able to afford one. Their church had paid for the wake and the hearse.

The priest had managed to get up money for a coffin. The city had, according to Ken's father, given Henri a pauper's grave.

No one, though, could afford a headstone. Those, his father had explained, cost too damned much.

Ken spotted the tree, walked to it, and then counted out eight steps to the tree's right. When he stopped, he squatted down and brushed aside the loose snow on the ground. It took him a few minutes to clear away enough to find the metal circle stamped with the number '98.'

That was Henri's plot number.

Ninety-eight.

The sound of rifle fire caused Ken to jump.

Ken's eyes locked onto an older man who stood at the position of attention a short distance away, his gaze focused across the cemetery. Ken turned and saw a trio of soldiers in dress uniform standing near the funeral he had seen coming into the cemetery.

As another volley was fired from the rifles, Ken straightened up and stood at the position of attention as well.

A final volley was fired, and then, from a short distance away, came the sound of a bugle playing taps.

Ken had heard it before, when his Uncle Tom had died, and it was a sad melody that pulled at him.

Taps faded away, and Ken relaxed. When he turned to look at the stranger again, he saw the man walking towards him. Ken took a nervous step back, prepared to run, and then he stopped when he recognized the man.

Dr. Leland, the librarian at the city library.

As Dr. Leland drew closer, the man took out a pair of half-glasses and set them on his nose.

"I thought that was you, Mr. Gunther," Dr. Leland exclaimed, pulling his right glove off his hand and proffering it.

Ken smiled, took off his mitten and shook the man's small, thin hand.

"A bit cold for a funeral, don't you think?" Dr. Leland asked, gesturing toward the burial that was finished.

"It's just cold," Ken stated.

Dr. Leland chuckled. "It most certainly is at that. Were you here for the funeral?"

Ken shook his head and gestured toward Henri's grave. "I came to say hi to my friend and to clear the snow off his medallion."

Dr. Leland turned slightly and peered down. In a soft voice, he said, "Ah, I see. May I ask who is buried here?"

"Henri Cristo," Ken replied.

"Oh, the boy who was killed by the drunk driver."

Ken nodded, not trusting his own voice. After a moment, he cleared his throat and asked, "Were you just walking through?"

Dr. Leland sighed. "No, not really. You see, that's my cousin they're burying. He drank himself to death."

"I'm sorry," Ken offered.

"No need to be, but thank you, Mr. Gunther." Dr. Leland slipped his gloved hands into his pockets and looked out across the graveyard. He sighed and shook his head.

"My cousin, he knew what he was doing," Dr. Leland stated. "He often said he lacked the courage to use a gun to finish himself off, but liquor was easy. Let me say, Mr. Gunther, that while it was easy for him, it was not easy for the rest of us. Well, I suppose that is neither here nor there at this point, hm?"

Dr. Leland looked down at his feet, then back up, as if searching for the words he wanted. After a moment of silence, he continued, his voice soft and his words spoken with care.

"His wife hated me in the end, and that's why I'm here instead of beside his grave," Dr. Leland informed him. "She doesn't want me anywhere near him, and that's her right. He was my cousin but the love of her life. She trumps me every time with that."

Ken looked at Dr. Leland with a hesitant frown. "What does trump mean?"

"Trump means that her love for him is more important than my familial relation to my cousin." The older man glanced down at Ken and let out a soft chuckle. "Hm, I suppose a statement like that deserves an explanation."

"I'm sorry," Ken said, his face flushing with embarrassment. "I didn't mean to interrupt."

"Nonsense," Dr. Leland replied, smiling. "You didn't know a word. You should always ask for clarification, Mr. Gunther. Now, what was I saying? Oh, yes. Explaining myself."

Ken waited, forgetting the cold and the funeral finishing beyond them.

"My cousin and I were inspired to join the Marines on December eighth, nineteen-forty-one," Dr. Leland stated. "That was the day after the attack on Pearl Harbor. Mind you, there were quite a few young men of equal mind. We saw that there were long lines for the Army and the Navy, and, well, being impetuous and impatient young men, we noticed the Marine Corps recruiter's door lacked any sort of line. So, in we went. Suffice it to say, we joined the Marine Corps, and in a few short months, we found ourselves heading off to war."

Dr. Leland looked down at the ground, nudged a stone free with the toe of his shoe and then continued his story. "Those were not, for the most part, pleasant days. The Japanese fought hard. We fought harder. They tortured the living and mutilated the dead. We returned the favor. We killed a great many men, my cousin and I, and we learned two important lessons on those islands. Do you know what they were?"

"No, sir," Ken replied.

"We learned I could kill without compunction," Dr. Leland said, his voice soft. "And we learned that my cousin could not. After the war, when we returned home, we went back about our lives. Or tried to. I had an easier time than he did. He began to drink. Heavily. His wife hated it, and it got to the point where he couldn't drink at home. Nor could he drink at any of the local establishments, either. His wife, well, let's say she's a powerful personality in her own right. People were afraid of her."

Dr. Leland smiled. "After a few years of this, my cousin would come to my house, and he would drink. Sometimes for days on end. His wife would send the police to my home, but I knew the officers and their families. These men knew what we had gone through in the Pacific, and so they did little more than confirm my cousin was alive, if not well. He killed himself by inches in my home, sitting across from me in my study. We never talked about the war. We never had to. It was always there between us."

"My father and his friends are kind of like that," Ken said in a low voice. "Sometimes they talk about Vietnam, but most of the time they don't."

"I am not surprised, Mr. Gunther," Dr. Leland replied. "It is that way with many veterans."

Dr. Leland paused, glanced over toward his cousin's funeral, then continued.

"In time, I moved the photos of us during the war out of the study. My war trophies and mementos, too. I hoped, too late, that the absence of these reminders might help slow his drinking. I needn't of worried about them. His reminders were in his head. He couldn't stop thinking of them. He drowned in alcohol, Mr. Gunther, and all I could do was watch him."

"Can alcohol kill someone?" Ken's voice came out small and weak in the cold air.

Dr. Leland looked at him, his eyes narrowed with concern. "Yes, in several ways. You know the first, don't you?"

Dr. Leland's gaze shifted for a moment to Henri's plot number and Ken nodded. "Yes, sir."

"Another way is through steady drinking. Day after day. Night after night. Years pile upon themselves. Eventually, you drown your organs in alcohol. And that is what my cousin did."

Dr. Leland cleared his throat. "I tried to save him, but he didn't want to be saved. I don't think his wife will ever understand that, and I certainly won't try to explain it. He didn't enjoy his drinking. He hated it, in fact. But it was all he could do to quiet the sounds of war, if only for a brief time."

"Do they stay?" Ken asked. "The sounds of war?"

"For some, Mr. Gunther, they never leave."

Dr. Leland turned and looked down at Ken, the man's face pained and serious.

"Some of us," Dr. Leland said in a low tone. "We can kill another man and never worry about everything that means. We don't worry about the ending of that life or how that affects the dead man's loved ones or his friends. All we do is move on to the next man and the next. It is a task we must do. Nothing more and nothing less.

"Then, Mr. Gunther, there are those for whom the taking of a life is a brutal, soul-tearing experience. They feel the death as keenly as though it was the death of a friend. They dwell upon the savagery of war, upon the nightmare they have poured into the life of another human's loved one. And this was my cousin, Mr. Gunther. This was what he thought of, day in and day out. He knew the true cost of war and paid the butcher's bill himself."

Dr. Leland looked back to the funeral. Cars were beginning to leave the cemetery, none of them driving too close to where Ken and the man stood. Finally, as the last vehicle exited and the cemetery's workers moved toward the open grave, Dr. Leland spoke again.

"I will leave you to your grief, Mr. Gunther." The man offered his hand again, and Ken shook it. "If you will forgive me, I would like to watch them bury my cousin. Perhaps we will meet here again. I suspect we both will be visiting our dead."

For a moment, Ken watched the retired librarian cross the cemetery toward the new grave. Then, he turned back to Henri's grave and squatted down.

For a moment, Ken remained silent. When he spoke, it was in a soft voice.

"I miss you, Henri," Ken said. "It's boring without you. I don't have anyone to play with. I miss hearing you laugh."

He sniffled, wiped his nose with his sleeve and cleared tears from his eyes. His father didn't like it when he cried.

When his sniffling was under control, Ken began to speak once more, telling his dead friend about books and the colonel and how much Henri's family missed him.

LEGO

"How's it going?"

Ken looked up and smiled at his father. "Good. I'm almost done."

"Oh yeah? Let me see what you got."

Ken picked up the half-finished Lego set.

His father chuckled. "What's that called again?"

"Um," Ken put down the set and looked at the box. "The Lunar Rocket Launcher."

"That the one you wanted?"

Ken nodded. "Bobby at school, he said it was the newest one."

"That's what the lady at the store said, too." His father smiled, lifted his beer and took a long drink. "I might be able to get my hands on a Lego catalog.

Thought if I did, maybe you'd look at it, pick some stuff out for Christmas."

"Really?" Ken asked, straightening up. "Could you really?"

"Yeah, Kid. Me and the lady at the store, we hit it off. She's easy on the eyes, and I told her about you. How you like to read and build, all that good stuff." His father shifted in his seat, finished his beer and set the empty on the coffee table. "She said if I get a list in to her, she can try and have the stuff in for Christmas. And if not for Christmas, definitely for your birthday in February."

"Wow," Ken whispered.

"I mean," his father continued, mustache twitching as he smiled, "it's going to be nineteen-eighty-six, and you're going to be twelve, so I don't know if you're going to be too big for toys. Maybe you just want a sweater or something."

"No!" Ken laughed. He got to his feet, went around the table and hugged his father. "Thank you."

His father kissed him on the forehead. "You're welcome. Love you, Kid. Now, go get me a beer, alright? Patriots are on in a bit, and I'm hoping Grogan'll be able to do something."

Ken nodded, picked up the empty bottle and carried it into the kitchen, his mind fixed firmly on Christmas and the possibility of more Lego sets.

FAMILY

"You seem rather off today, Mr. Gunther," Colonel Essex stated. "Is everything alright with you?"

Ken put his teacup down, kicked his legs a little to let his boots swing above the floor, and then answered, "No. Not really."

Colonel Essex set his own teacup down on its saucer and asked, "May I inquire as to what it is that's bothering you so?"

Ken cleared his throat before he nodded. "We're going to see my grandfather tonight."

"Your father's father, I assume?" the man asked with a raised eyebrow.

"Yes."

"Do you dislike your grandfather?" Colonel Essex asked, a strangely serious tone to his voice.

"No," Ken answered after a moment. "I mean, I don't really like him too much either. He's, I don't know, strict? He usually tells me I'm not man enough. I have to eat more and get bigger."

"Ah," Colonel Essex nodded. "I have heard men such as your grandfather referred to as 'the salt of the earth' before, Master Gunther, and I can assure you that is not the case. Be that as it may, however, I must ask, is there anything I can do for you?"

Ken shook his head before he picked up a cookie off the plate. Tea and chocolate cookies had become a Friday afternoon staple. Thursday's he ate with the Cristos, and Friday evening were his father's game nights. Sometimes Lee came over on Sundays to sit in silence and watch the Patriots play, but most often Ken and his father were alone.

Ken's grandfather didn't like the city they lived in, so he didn't come to visit.

Ken didn't mind.

"Mr. Gunther," Colonel Essex said, his voice low and soft with concern. "Are you quite certain you don't want to avoid the visit?"

Ken smiled. "I have to. My Dad says family is an obligation. My grandfather called up last night and asked my Dad to come over. My grandfather will want to see me. Talk about how skinny I am and about how I have to eat more."

Colonel Essex's lips became thin but he refrained from speaking for a moment.

When he did speak, it was in a pleasant manner. "I am sorry your grandfather speaks to you in such a way, Master Gunther. There are many such men like him. They are of the opinion that brutality builds men. I am not. When do you leave?"

"After my Dad gets home from work," Ken stated. "He'll shower and then we'll go."

Colonel Essex glanced up at the long, dark wood clock on his mantle. "That seems to give us about an hour, Mr. Gunther. I know I promised you I would teach you backgammon. Would you like to start now?"

Ken grinned and nodded.

Colonel Essex chuckled. "The set is by the bust of Caesar near the right of the door. It's a small leather case. Bring it here, my young friend, and I shall teach you a game said to drive sultans mad."

Ken slid out of his chair and hurried toward the game, thoughts of his grandfather and the long ride to

the man's home fading beneath his excitement for
backgammon.

GRANDFATHER

They went into the city, the pickup rumbling over rough spots in the road, Ken's father muttering and cursing with each thump the truck suffered through.

"Give me a cigarette, Kid."

Ken took a fresh pack of Lucky Strikes out of the glovebox, tore off the cellophane wrapper, and shook a cigarette out. He handed it to his father and pushed in the truck's lighter.

His father chuckled as he tucked the cigarette between his lips and ruffled Ken's hair. "You're a smart kid. You take after your grandfather, that's for damned sure."

His father lapsed back into silence, and Ken remained quiet, as he had for much of the forty-five-minute drive.

The lighter clicked, popped, and his father plucked it out, deftly lighting his cigarette with it. The man rolled down the window and exhaled through his nose, the breeze carrying the smoke out into the cold evening air.

"Put the radio on, Kid."

Ken did so, a news program crackling into life. He didn't pay attention to it. Instead, Ken looked out his window at the way the pickup traveled from streetlight to streetlight on the long road. As he watched, the lights flickered into life. Beyond them, the sky deepened. It would be close to full dark when they reached his grandfather's house, and Ken wondered how the old man would be.

Ken glanced at his father and saw the subtle hints of anxiety around his eyes and the long, harsh drags he took on the cigarette.

Ken slipped his hands into the pockets of his zip-up sweatshirt and focused on the road once more. The miles rolled past, his father smoking an additional cigarette, fishing it out of the pack himself.

Ken watched darkness absorb the land on either side and soon, the lights of houses could be seen. His father turned on the directional and guided the pickup onto the right branch of a long fork in the road, and they entered the outskirts of the city. As the truck slowed and stopped at various intersections and they traveled deeper into the city, Ken caught glimpses of other people's lives.

From his seat, Ken saw the flicker of television sets and people eating dinner. Some closed their blinds and curtains as he passed by, performing rituals he knew nothing of.

He saw mothers and fathers, children and relations.

All of them looked happy.

"Almost there, Kid," his father sighed.

Ken shifted his attention to his father, who sat rigid in his seat. In the glow of the streetlights and truck's dashboard lights, Ken saw the white-knuckle grip his father had on the Dodge's steering wheel.

His father flashed him a tight grin, smoothed out his mustache and nodded, repeating, "Almost there."

They turned onto Myrtle Street, pulled up to the low, ramshackle house, and Ken's father shifted the truck park and turned the engine off.

"Okay, Kid, let's do this."

Ken unbuckled and climbed out of the truck. The cold air caused him to shiver, and for a moment, he struggled with closing the door. A glance at the house showed a shape in the window, so Ken threw his slight weight against the door, forcing it closed as his father stepped around the front of the truck and onto the sidewalk.

Ken's father gave a curt nod of approval, and they walked side by side up the narrow path to the front door. As their feet touched the bottom stair, the door opened, and Ken's grandfather greeted them.

"Boys," the older man said, the cigarette between his lips dancing and flicking ash onto the concrete steps. "You made good time."

The old man extended his hand, and after his father had shaken it, Ken did the same. He kept his face neutral and returned as much pressure as he could as his grandfather squeezed Ken's hand.

The old man grinned and let go. "You're starting to shake hands like a man, Boy. Good. Come on in."

Ken slipped his throbbing hand into his pocket and followed the man into the small house.

His grandfather closed the door and ushered them into the small front room. The worn and polished furniture was rearranged as it always was. Ken could not remember a time when the furniture remained in place from one visit to the next.

Ken sat down in the hard, cane-back chair reserved for him, put his hands on his lap, and glanced at the walls. The photographs and paintings of dogs playing cards were in new and curious patterns. Ken tried to follow the thought process that dictated where each item should go, but he stopped when his grandfather began speaking.

"Beer, Mike?"

"Yeah, Pops," Ken's father answered, sitting down in an easy chair, the springs groaning with the man's weight.

"Put on a few pounds?" the older man asked.

Ken's father offered a grunt in response.

His grandfather looked over to Ken, asking, "Milk?"

"Yes, sir."

The old man nodded and went into the kitchen. Ken's father smoothed out his mustache.

From the kitchen came the pop and rattle of bottle caps onto the counter. Ken's grandfather returned a moment later, holding two bottles by their necks in one hand and a small carton of milk in the other.

Ken accepted the milk. "Thank you, sir."

"You're welcome. Stopped at the corner store for it today. Don't drink it myself. No need."

By the time the old man turned away, Ken saw the milk carton was open.

Ken blinked, surprised at the sight of it. He wouldn't sit and struggle with breaking the seal while his grandfather watched, there would be no growing disappointment as Ken fought with the waxed cardboard.

When Ken glanced up, he saw his grandfather pass off one of the bottles to his father.

Ken sipped the cold, sweet milk as his grandfather sat down. The old man took a long pull from the bottle, sighed, and spoke in German.

Ken's father stiffened, nodded, and said to Ken, "Why don't you go upstairs to my old room?"

"Ken," his grandfather added. "You can go in the closet. My uniform's in there. Take a look at it. Don't touch anything else, though."

"Yes, sir." Ken stood up, set his milk on a small side table, and left the room. The worn boards of the hallway creaked and groaned in unfamiliar ways as he walked. Some of the noises were abrupt, others drawn out, but all were disturbing. Ken imagined ghosts and monsters springing from the floor. When he reached the stairwell, he stopped and turned on the light.

The narrow flight of stairs curved up and out of sight. Each step dipped toward the center, thinned and worn by decades of use. Above him, the light faded and flared up, leaving Ken blinking and grasping for the thin, smooth banister that helped guide him to the second floor.

When he reached the upper level, he heard his father's voice, then his grandfather's, but the words they spoke were indecipherable. For a moment, Ken paused, then he continued to his father's boyhood room. Ken stepped across the threshold into the room and turned on the light.

Only a few pieces of furniture occupied the room. Ken saw a chair with a broken leg, a bureau missing two of its five drawers, and an old record player. To the left of the room stood the closed door of the closet.

It was a place normally forbidden to him.

Too much of the past, his father told him. The death of an aunt Ken had never known, the passing of his grandmother, who was a mystery still.

A sense of unease rose in Ken's chest and nestled there. He tried to understand why his grandfather would give him permission to enter the closet, but Ken's curiosity and longing silenced his inner questioning and spurred him into movement.

He walked across the room carefully, glancing back and half-expecting his grandfather to appear in the doorway and rescind the offer.

But no one came to stop him.

Ken opened the closet door, reached up for the pull chain of the light, and turned it on.

The light flared into life, illuminating the dress uniform standing there. Along with the uniform, there was something new. A short bureau with a large piece of folded red cloth upon it. Curious, Ken picked up the cloth, the fabric rough beneath his fingers. It smelled faintly of cedar, a scent he knew well from the cedar closet in his and his father's bedroom.

Carefully, Ken unfolded the cloth and found himself holding a large flag with a swastika on it. There were holes and dark stains in it. After a moment of holding it, Ken folded the flag back the way it had been, and when he went to set it back down he saw the flag had been resting on a wooden cigar box.

Curious, Ken set the flag off to one side and opened the large box.

Within it, he found a pistol he knew to be a Luger resting atop some papers and a few photographs. He had seen similar weapons in books on World War Two. The pistol's barrel rested on a small, dark booklet stained and frayed around the edges. The word upon it was difficult to read. As he looked closer, Ken realized the word was written in a different language.

Intrigued, Ken picked up the booklet and opened it. He found himself looking at a photograph of a young man.

"You're a strange boy, Ken."

Ken jerked around and saw his grandfather. The man stood just inside the room, a fresh bottle of beer in hand. His grandfather flashed one of his rare smiles. "I know every board that creaks in this house. Can make my way through it without making a sound. Used to scare the hell out of your father.

"Now," his grandfather continued, "if you were your father, you'd be holding that Luger like you were Jesse James. But you picked up the book."

"Is it a book, sir?" Ken asked, glancing down at it.

His grandfather nodded and took a drink. "Oh, that it is. A damned important one, too."

The old man crossed the room on surprisingly silent feet. He held out his hand, and Ken placed the book in it.

"I took this off a German I killed outside of a little 'berg in Germany." His grandfather sipped at his beer. "It was hard, Ken. I was twenty years old. Turns out he was eighteen. His camouflage had been good. I never saw him in the snow. Not until he moved. Just a moment too soon."

Ken watched his grandfather thumb open the book.

"His name was Rolfe," the old man sighed. "I had to use my knife, Ken. It was damned hard. I don't think anyone can tell you what it's going to be like when you stab a man to death."

Ken remained silent, his eyes upon his grandfather, whose features softened as he spoke.

"I don't know why I took the book and his papers, his photos," his grandfather closed the book and stared at it. "A few years ago, I got in touch with some guys in the German army. They helped me try to find

Rolfe's family. I wanted to mail this back to them. Kind of say I was sorry for having killed their boy."

Ken's grandfather shook his head, then took another, longer drink from the bottle.

"The family was dead," the old man continued. "Dead from a bombing run a few days before I killed the boy. I doubt he knew about it. I'm sure he thought they were alive. I tried to take comfort in that. I tried for a long time."

Ken's grandfather handed him the book.

"It's his soldier's book," the old man explained as Ken returned it to the spot he had taken it from. "It tells us everything about him as a soldier. He was more than that, though. He was someone's baby boy."

Ken's grandfather sighed and finished his beer.

"We were all something more before the war, Ken. Trouble is, sometimes, we can't remember what that was."

Ken's grandfather turned off the lights and led the way out of the room.

PIZZA

Ken struggled under the weight of the paper bag, but he didn't let his father know. His father was focused on walking up the steps while carrying a pair of large pizzas and a handle of whiskey.

From the Cristos' apartment came the squawking of hens, and the cadence of Mama Cristo's voice lifted up in prayer. Ken's father shook his head as they passed the door.

"Praying doesn't do anything," he muttered, glancing over his shoulder at Ken. "God doesn't care one way or the other."

His father's words were slightly slurred, and there was a tint of anger in them.

Ken suspected work hadn't been good. His father usually didn't buy whiskey or pizza in the middle of the week.

When they reached their apartment door, his father put his shoulder into it and pushed. The old lock popped, and they went in, the door bouncing off the wall. His father stopped it with an elbow and continued to the kitchen. Once there, he set the pizza down on the small, two-burner stove and the whiskey on the countertop.

"Put the beer on the table, Kid."

Ken did so, his arms relieved to be freed from the weight of the two six-packs in the bag.

"Get me a beer."

Taking hold of the paper bag, Ken tore it down one seam as he had seen his father do. When the six-packs were revealed, he took one of the bottles out and twisted the cap off before placing both on the table.

His father chuckled. "Good boy. You want one or two slices?"

"Two, please," Ken answered, even though he only wanted one. His father would push a second one, and he wouldn't be pleasant about it if he had more whiskey than beer.

Ken's father nodded his approval and ripped the top of the pizza box off, and then tore the top in half. He put a pair of slices on one half and handed it to Ken. "Put that in the front room, Kid, and then grab yourself a Coke, okay?"

"Okay."

Ken did as he was told, and by the time he returned to the kitchen, his father had piled four slices onto the other half of the pizza box top. He had also finished the beer Ken had opened.

"Pop another one for me."

Ken did so and handed it to him before getting a bottle of Coke out of the fridge. They walked into the front room and sat down on the couch together.

"Do you want me to put the news on?" Ken asked.

His father shook his head, took a bite of pizza and followed it with a drink of beer. "Nah. I don't need any more bad news."

Ken looked at his father, confused.

The man sighed. "Your grandfather died this morning."

Ken blinked. "How?"

For a moment, his father hesitated. "He went into the closet, got his Luger out, and shot himself in the head."

"Why?"

"Cancer," his father answered and finished his beer. "That's what he wanted to tell me last time we were there. Didn't want to say it over the phone."

Ken put his pizza down and wiped at his eyes.

"Don't cry, Kid," his father told him, his voice soft but firm. "No need to cry. Dead is dead. I've told you that before."

Ken held back the tears, picked up his pizza once more, and took a bite. In the stillness of the room, he chewed his food and stared at the television's blank screen.

REFLECTIONS

"I am sorry to hear of your grandfather's passing, Mr. Gunther." Colonel Essex spoke in a low, comforting tone. "It is, as you are painfully aware, I know, difficult to lose a loved one."

Ken swallowed hard and nodded, blinking away the tears that threatened to spill from his eyes.

Colonel Essex frowned. "Master Gunther, if you feel the need to cry, then by all means cry. I will not think less of you if you weep for the dead."

"My father says dead is dead. There's no need to cry," Ken replied, his voice nothing more than a hoarse whisper.

"Ah."

They sat in silence for a short time. Finally, Ken wiped at his eyes and forced a smile.

"Mr. Gunther," Colonel Essex began. "You do not have to stand on ceremony for me. We are friends, young man, and I am quite pleased for it. If you do not wish to speak of your grandfather's passing, we shall not. We can focus our attention on books and backgammon, tea and cookies."

"Books and backgammon, and tea and cookies," Ken said, his smile more relaxed.

"Very good. Did you finish *Captain's Courageous*?"

Ken nodded. "It was really good. I liked Harvey. Not at first, he was really, I don't know. A spoiled brat?"

Colonel Essex laughed and clapped his hands together. "Yes. Yes! Kipling made Harvey a spoiled brat. Otherwise, how could he grow while he was on the *We're Here*? It is a plain story of a young man's growth from the spoiled brat of a millionaire to a young man firmly rooted in the realities of the world, and who has been forged into a man by his experiences at sea. I am so glad you enjoyed it, Master Gunther. Do you think you're ready for another?"

"Yes, sir." Ken nodded eagerly, leaning forward.

"All right then." Colonel Essex leaned forward in a conspiratorial way. "It is a book called *The Pearl* and it is, at times, difficult. Far more so than the others you have read. Not for language, mind you. Not at all. No, it is for the ideas that are put forward. The thoughts that you will find racing through your mind as you turn from page to page. It is not a war story, not in the sense you are familiar with, but it is, nonetheless, a tale of violence and greed and desperation. Do you think, Master Gunther, that this might be something you would be willing to read?"

The description had left Ken breathless and he could only nod in reply.

"Excellent," Colonel Essex said with a wink. "Now, my young friend, fetch the backgammon board and prepare to suffer ignominious defeat at my hands."

Snickering, Ken got up and retrieved the back-gammon set. As he did so, the door to the library opened and Mrs. Dunne entered carrying her tray of cookies and the tea service.

Ken waved, sat down and opened the game.

KEN'S FATHER

Ken sat in the cab of the truck, staring out at the world as his father pulled into the gas station. Yawning, Ken made sure his father couldn't see how tired he was.

The truck came to a rough stop at one of the two fuel pumps, and his father shut the engine off. The man sat still for a moment, bleary-eyed and staring out the windshield as snow fell beyond the steel canopy of the gas station. His father kept one hand on the wheel and the other on the keys. The engine ticked and coughed as it cooled, and Ken waited.

"Cigarette."

Ken took the pack off the dashboard, removed one cigarette and found his father's lighter. He passed both to the man, who grunted his thanks.

The interior of the truck stank of whiskey and beer, and a moment later, fresh smoke joined the mixture. His father blinked, tossed the lighter onto the bench seat and then rolled the driver's side window down a few inches.

"Ken," his father muttered.

"Yes?"

"We at a full service?"

Ken looked out his own window, shrunk back slightly and answered, "No."

"Fuck."

Ken relaxed a fraction. "Do you want me to go have them put some money on the pump?"

"Huh? What?" his father tapped the head of the cigarette off into the open ashtray. "Nah. I'll do it. In a minute."

The last few words were slurred, and his father's eyelids drooped.

Ken waited.

The man blinked, looked around, and then straightened up. "We at a full service?"

"No."

Anger flared up on his father's face. "'Course not."

"Want me to go put some money on the pump?"

His father looked at him, then he dug out his wallet. "Yeah. Tell 'em to put five on it. That'll be enough to get us home. Should've just stayed at Dave's tonight."

"Uncle Dave got arrested for knocking out Aunt Wanda," Ken reminded him.

"What?" His father shook his head. "Damn. Don't remember that. Wanda kick us out?"

Ken nodded.

"'Cause I brought the whiskey?"

"Yes."

"Huh. Bitch," his father sighed. "Hate women. Good for nothin'."

Ken waited in silence as his father fished a five-dollar bill out of the wallet and passed it over. When he took it, Ken asked, "Do you need cigarettes?"

His father picked up the pack, squinted, and answered, "Nah. Got a carton at home. I should be good."

"Okay."

Ken unbuckled and got out of the truck. He checked both ways and then trudged across the narrow strip of snow-covered asphalt to the door of the station. A bell rang, and when he went inside, a young black man looked up from a magazine.

"Hey, little man," the attendant said, grinning and putting his magazine down. "What'll it be on this cheery December night?"

"Five dollars of regular, please," Ken answered, handing the money over.

"Cool, cool," the attendant replied, accepting the cash and ringing up the sale. He glanced over at the truck. "You with your dad or your mom?"

"My dad," Ken said. "He's finishing a smoke before he puts any gas in."

"I appreciate that," the attendant smiled. He tore off the receipt and passed it to Ken. "Have a good night, and be safe. Weatherman is saying we got a few more inches coming in."

"Thank you, and you be safe too." Ken waved goodbye and left the station, the attendant picking up his magazine.

Ken followed his own footsteps back to the truck, opened the gas cap and then struggled with the nozzle. He slid the pump mechanism up, squeezed the cold metal of the handle with both hands and watched the numbers roll by on the counter. When the pump shut off, Ken gave the handle a good shake, just as his father had shown him, and then put the nozzle back in its holder. Ken eased screwed the gas cap into place and then he opened the door and climbed in.

The back of his father's head rested against the rear window, his eyes closed, cigarette still held loosely between his lips. The head of ash on the cigarette was long, and without disturbing his father, Ken reached across and took the cigarette out of his mouth. He stubbed the butt out and left it in the ashtray. When he finished, he closed the door, and his father woke up.

His father blinked. "You pay and pump?"

Ken nodded.

"Good boy," his father murmured. He was about to say more when a small, two-door car pulled into the gas station and parked at the pump directly in front of them. A moment later, the doors opened, pair of young Asian men stepped out and Ken stiffened.

"What the hell?" his father hissed.

The young men talked to each other in a language Ken didn't understand, and the passenger went into the station while the driver stepped around to the pump.

And while Ken didn't know what they had said, his father did.

A look of pure rage filled his father's face as he threw open the door and climbed out. Ken watched, his heart racing as his father took a step toward the other car. His father's hands were clenched into fists, the wind whipping his long black hair, the bright lights of the gas station illuminating the mask of hatred that settled onto his father's face.

The young man at the other pump looked up, and fear stamped itself on his face.

Ken watched as the young man raised a hand in greeting, a nervous smile fighting the fear, but the smile froze, half-formed as Ken's father spoke.

Words Ken had never heard before raced from his father's mouth. Smooth and sibilant, graceful and elegant, despite the venom with which Ken's father spoke them.

"Tôi đã giết cha mẹ của bạn! Tôi đã giết ông bà của bạn! Tôi sẽ giết bạn!" All traces of drunkenness were gone from his father's voice.

Movement caught Ken's eye, and when he turned his head to the right, he saw the other young man hurry out of the station. Ken's father raised his voice, pointing first at the young man at the fuel pump, then at his companion.

The man beside the car remained where he was, his Adam's apple bobbing as his companion moved closer to him. In a moment, the two young men were shoulder to shoulder, eyes fixed on Ken's father, unwilling to look away. Ken watched as his father gestured wildly, his voice becoming deep with a fury Ken had rarely seen and one he feared when it did.

He shivered in the truck, eyes darting from his father to the young men, from the young men to the station, where the attendant stood in the doorway. The attendant held his magazine in his hands, his expression one of surprise and fear. Ken saw the indecision on the man's face, his uncertainty.

Ken listened and watched and shrank into the safety of the seat while his father's tirade continued until it devolved into a single, repeated phrase.

"Tôi sẽ giết bạn! Tôi sẽ giết bạn! Tôi sẽ giết bạn! Tôi sẽ giết bạn!"

The young man finished pumping the gas and dropped the nozzle twice before his companion took it from him and returned it to the pump. Without taking their eyes off his father, the young men got into their car, started the engine and backed the vehicle away.

Ken's father followed them.

Every step was stiff, as though his rage sought to explode from his flesh. He gestured wildly, screamed at them and came to a stop just outside of the cover of the steel canopy. Snow clung to his long black hair and to the battered, brown leather jacket he wore. Ken's father howled as the young men pulled out of the gas station and onto the street. When the red brake lights were no longer in sight, Ken's father turned around and returned to the truck.

The attendant remained in the doorway, watching. He no longer had a magazine in his hands, but a baseball bat, the head of it wrapped in silver duct tape.

Ken's father climbed back in the truck, slamming the door behind him. He gripped the steering wheel with both hands, his teeth clenched, breath rushing through them. His wild eyes refused to remain on any one object.

"I hate 'em, Ken," his father hissed.

Ken waited and watched.

"Fuckin' bastards," his father continued. "I told 'em I hate 'em. Hate all of 'em. I told them I probably killed their parents. Probably killed everyone in their goddamned families. If I had my way, Ken, I'd kill those fuckers, too. Right here. Kick 'em right down to the fucking pavement and blow their fuckin' brains out. It's what you do. You don't take prisoners. You never take prisoners."

His father started the engine of the truck, looked at Ken and asked, "Do you understand?"

"Yes, sir," Ken whispered. "You never take prisoners."

"Never."

His father shifted the truck into drive and left the station, the attendant still in the doorway, magazine in hand.

Ken remained pressed against the door and tried not to imagine his father killing the young men.

TREASURE ISLAND

They sat in a room Colonel Essex referred to as the parlor.

Ken wasn't sure what a parlor was, but he liked it. The room had a pair of large leather chairs, several floor lamps, a pair of tables for each chair, and bookcases.

Tall, beautiful bookcases made from dark wood with glass doors and brass hinges. Here and there stood photographs of Colonel Essex and various members of the Colonel's family.

But for the most part, the bookcases were filled with books. Ken was fairly certain there were more books in the Colonel's parlor than there were in his school's library.

Ken sat in one of the leather chairs, and Colonel Essex occupied the other, the man's wheelchair tucked off to one side. On the table to the colonel's left was a small, silver bell. Ken knew from experience that if the Colonel needed anything, he had only to ring the bell, and the woman who occasionally worked for him would come into the room.

The Colonel rarely rang it.

Empty teacups and small plates decorated with the crumbs of recently finished cookies stood on the table tops as well. In his hands, Ken held a new book. The book was bound in soft brown leather, the title and the author's name stamped in gold upon the cover.

"I read *Treasure Island* when I was your age," Colonel Essex informed him.

Ken ran his hands over the leather and let his fingers trace the words. "This is really cool."

Colonel Essex offered a wry smile. "'Really cool'?"

Ken nodded.

"Slang is always adapting," the old man murmured. "Nevertheless, you like it?"

"Yes," Ken smiled. "How long may I borrow it?"

"Borrow? No, it is a gift, much like *Moby Dick*," Colonel Essex smiled. "I think it fitting that since you have Nathaniel's favorite book, well, you should have mine as well."

"This was your copy?" Ken asked, surprised.

"Oh yes. Open the book."

Ken did so and saw handwriting. The letters for each word were long and beautiful, giving each word a grace Ken had not seen before. Leaning forward, he read the message.

To my dearest Grandson, I hope you will enjoy this short tale as much as I did. Love always, Grandmother.

December the 25th, 1911.

Ken realized he had been holding his breath and let it out slowly. "How old is the book?"

"Turn the page once more," Colonel Essex said gently.

Ken did so and whistled. "Wow, eighteen-eighty-three."

"That is not the original binding, I'm afraid," the man confessed. "I was rather rough with the book at times. When I grew older, I had it rebound. I am hopeful you will enjoy the book as my grandmother and I did."

"I will," Ken whispered, closing the book. "Thank you so much."

"You are quite welcome, Mr. Gunther," Colonel Essex replied, straightening up. "You will keep it safe, I trust?"

"Yes," Ken nodded his head.

"Good. Now, tell me, what are you learning in school?"

"Math," Ken grumbled, tightening his grip on the book.

"Ah, yes. You have a rather confrontational relationship with math, do you not?" Colonel Essex asked with an understanding smile.

"Yes," Ken admitted.

Colonel Essex peered at him for a moment and then asked, "Mr. Gunther, when we're playing backgammon, do you know what to do when you roll, say, a six and a one?"

Ken frowned at the question. "I can take a point. Usually."

"That you can," Colonel Essex nodded. "If you were to be so dastardly as to hit one of my men and put him on the bar, would you be careful to leave a point open for him to return?"

"Of course," Ken stated.

"How would you figure all of this out, Mr. Gunther?"

"I count the spaces and then make sure I can cover my men before I decide to hit you," Ken explained.

"Ah. I see. You count the spaces."

Silence filled the room for a moment as Colonel Essex smiled at him.

Understanding rushed over Ken and he felt his cheeks redden with embarrassment.

"No need for shame, Master Gunther. None at all," Colonel Essex said gently. "Sometimes it helps to put everything into perspective. Now, I have been meaning to ask and please, if you don't wish to discuss it tell me, but I was wondering how you've been doing since your grandfather's passing."

Holding the book in his lap, Ken hesitated. Then, in a faltering voice he whispered, "It reminds me of Henri."

"I thought it might. Why don't you fetch the backgammon set? I'll ring Mrs. Dunne for more tea, and we can talk about your memories, alright?"

Ken nodded, held onto the book a moment longer, and then rose to his feet as Colonel Essex rang the bell.

BUCKY DAY

Sitting in the corner of the Quonset hut that served as his father's office, Ken huddled beneath an old wool blanket, the heater glowing orange and crackling close by. From out in the yard, he heard the clang and scrape of metal, the roar of a diesel engine, and the profane language of his father and the men who worked under him.

Ken nestled in deeper, enjoying the rough feel of the wool. It reminded him of his father's mustache, as did the faint odor of cigarettes and coffee that wafted up from the fabric. From beneath the blanket's folds, Ken retrieved the copy of *Treasure Island* Colonel Essex had given him. For a moment, he held the book with no small amount of reverence. When he opened it, there would be a different smell. The smell of pipe tobacco. Cherry.

Colonel Essex had told him it had been his brother's favorite flavor, and after the war, he had smoked his pipe whenever he had read the book, which was often. Over the years, the smell had never faded, and Colonel Essex believed there was some small part of his brother that lingered on between the covers because of the smoke. Colonel Essex's brother was, the old man had said, forever with Long John Silver, Jim, and Captain Smollett, searching for the treasure.

The hinges of the office door screamed in protest as it opened, a gust of bitter, January wind nearly tearing it from the hands of the large man who ducked to enter the building. As the door closed, the man unwrapped a thick scarf from around his lower face and removed the dark blue watchman's cap he wore.

Ken closed the book and smiled in greeting.

Bucky Day, the head of security for the lower portion of the base, worked his jaw back and forth before catching sight of Ken.

"Hey!" Bucky laughed, striding forward and extending his hand. "Mike didn't tell me he brought you in today."

Ken shook the offered hand, his own vanishing into the midst of Bucky's. Ken had known Bucky for as long as he could remember.

"No school today?" Bucky sat down in one of the old office chairs, the springs groaning as he did so.

"No, Bucky. Too much snow again. Dad said he couldn't miss today."

"Yeah, he's right about that," Bucky put his boots up on an overturned milkcrate, snow and clumps of salt dropping off. "We had to offload the batteries from one of the attack subs. Commander wasn't going to let a boat just sit in the yard. Not 'cause of some damned snow. Hey, watcha readin' this time?"

"*Treasure Island*." Ken held up the book.

Bucky laughed and shook his head. "Too many words in there that I don't know. I looked at it once when I was in the hospital. Nurses figured since I was going to be there for a while, I ought to have something to keep me busy. I had something to keep me busy, though. You know what that was?"

Ken shook his head.

Bucky winked. "Watching the nurses walk by."

Ken snickered, and the man let out a laugh.

"Yeah, I was there for a long, long time." He rubbed at his jaw again and sighed. "I hate the cold."

The door opened again, and a middle-aged Asian woman stepped in. Ken recognized her as one of the women who took the food orders. A smile started on her face, but it froze when she saw Bucky.

Bucky's pleasant expression vanished as he snatched an old tin mug off Ken's father's desk and hurled it at the woman, who ducked the object, trying to get back out of the hut.

"What did I tell you about any of you coming near me?" Bucky bellowed, the walls shaking and reverberating with the power of his lungs as he looked for another item to throw.

Before he found it, the woman got the door open and raced out.

"I hate 'em," Bucky swore. "Hate all of 'em. Your father knows. He understands. I wouldn't let 'em on the base if it was up to me."

Bucky worked his jaw up and down and left to right.

"They're the reason I was in the hospital," Bucky grumbled. "Months of my life in there. Listening to men scream and beg to die. And every time it gets cold, every time it's nasty weather, I feel it. All this. All of it."

The man touched his jaw, and for the first time, Ken saw a thin scar that ran the length of Bucky's jaw. It started at the left ear and followed the jawline down to the chin. The mark was pale white, standing out against the red of the man's still flush face.

"Sixteen years old," Bucky said, glancing back at the door. "Joined the Army. Helped retake Guam. I was driving a jeep for my sergeant, and we were ambushed. I was hit in the stomach, and he was killed right off the bat. Bang. All done. I tried to crawl on the beach, but I just couldn't do it. Finally, after an hour or so, this Japanese soldier comes along. I begged him for help. Begged him. Instead, he bayonetted me six times, then shot me in the face."

Bucky opened his mouth and removed a set of false teeth. He clacked them at Ken before putting them back in.

"Some Marines, they found me. Saved me," Bucky continued. "I wouldn't hate the Japanese if they had just shot me. Not at all. But they didn't just shoot me.

That bastard took his time. He'd put the tip of the bayonet against my stomach and then just push real slow. I didn't scream after the first one. Nope. That's what he wanted, and I wasn't goin' to give the fucker that."

Ken felt his eyes widen and suddenly he pictured Bucky stretched out on a beach. The thought tore at him and caused his throat to tighten. A shiver gripped his spine and caused him to clench his teeth. He tried to push away the unwanted image but couldn't.

Bucky broke the spell a moment later as he spoke again. With a shake of his head, Bucky continued. "I had a lot of time to think in the hospital. They had to put a steel jaw in, that's why it hurts when it's cold out. Fake teeth. Had to learn how to talk again. Chew again. Lots of time to think. I would walk around the hospital and look at the guys who would never walk again. Some who weren't men anymore. Guys who were blind or deaf, or both. That's when I realized the Japanese were monsters. All of them. Every single person in that part of the world. Hell, they wouldn't be missed at all. Your father knows. Hell, if he doesn't —"

Ken held his breath and waited.

Bucky sighed, smiled and said, "Where'd you get that book anyway? Your father?"

"No, Bucky," Ken answered, and he told him about Colonel Essex.

THE FLAG

The flag lay folded into a triangle on the table.

Beside it stood a half-finished handle of whiskey.

Ken crossed the room and looked at the flag, confused as to why there would be one in the house. He only ever saw them at the base and at school. After a moment, he reached out and touched the rough fabric. The stars were stitched on, the raised threads a smooth contrast against his fingertips.

From the front room came the familiar whir and click of his father's lighter.

Ken put his schoolbag on the floor under the kitchen table and then made his way to the front room, where his father sat in his chair. The ashtray on the coffee table was full of cigarette butts, the tall glass beside it nearly empty. His father's eyes were half-closed, a fresh cigarette dangling from his lips, and the lighter held loosely in one hand.

As Ken stepped into the room, his father's eyes focused on him.

"Kid," his father murmured. "Gonna have you go to the Cristos' in a minute. 'Kay?"

Ken nodded.

His father, Ken realized, had on a suit. The man's normally untamed hair had been smoothed out and pulled into a ponytail. Even his mustache was trimmed. His father wore a pair of dress shoes instead of work boots. Dried mud clung to the sides of the shoes.

Ken's father took a long drag off the cigarette, tilted his head back and blew the smoke toward the ceiling before he let out a sharp, angry laugh.

"Planted my old man today, Kid," his father sighed, slowly lifting his head back up. His eyes wandered for a moment. "Buried him in Middletown today."

"Oh." Ken didn't know what else to say. He put his hands in his pockets. Tears welled up in his eyes.

"Didn't want you to see that, Kid," his father mumbled around the cigarette. "Didn't need to. 'Kay?"

Ken nodded and sniffled back the tears.

"Was just a box," his father continued. "No open casket. Blew his fuckin' brains out. Christ. Asshole."

Ken's father leaned forward, picked up the glass after several tries, and finished the whiskey. "Go to Cristos'. I get you tomorrow. Sober. Right?"

"Yeah," Ken said, and he left the room. He paused in the doorway to the kitchen, the sadness clenching his chest.

He didn't know why he was sad.

Ken glanced into the kitchen, and his eyes fell on the flag and the whiskey. For a heartbeat, he thought about a drink. Thought maybe it would help.

An image of his father swearing at the gas station destroyed any idea of whiskey.

With his shoulders slumped, Ken went to the bedroom and gathered up what he would need for a night with the Cristos'.

NURSE TESSIER

Ken's jaw hurt as he sat in the chair, arms folded over his chest and his heart thumping hard.

The nurse's office smelled of disinfectant and reminded him of hospitals and death. He remembered being at Backus Hospital, when his father had brought him and the Cristos to the hospital after the ambulance had rushed Henri to the emergency room. Ken could remember Henri's blood drying on the floor, the wheels of the ambulance's gurney leaving trails of it behind.

Ken pushed the memories away and lowered his arms, he stretched them out and looked at his hands. His knuckles were red and scraped, the fingers throbbing. Blood had settled into the lines of his fingers, and he could see some of the skin torn up in thin strips pushed back upon itself.

The door to the office opened, and Ken looked up.

Principal Hogan walked in with a nurse who wasn't Ms. Coker, the regular school nurse. Ken started to stand up, and the principal shook his head.

"Sit down, Ken," Mr. Hogan said, and Ken did so. "What happened?"

Ken cleared his throat. "Greg told me he was glad Henri was dead."

Mr. Hogan frowned. "Anything else?"

Ken hesitated.

"Ken?"

Ken's shoulders sagged, and he whispered, "Greg said the only good—"

Mr. Hogan held up a hand. "That's enough, Ken, you don't have to say it. That's a terrible word. Yes, that's what a few of the other students heard, too. Alright, I have to call your father. You'll need to have your hands looked at, and you'll be suspended for a day."

Ken nodded.

"Ms. Tessier will help you. She's filling in for Ms. Coker, who's out this week." Mr. Hogan paused and then added, "Ken, I'm sorry Greg said those things to you. I shouldn't say this, but he'll be suspended for much longer than you."

Without anything else, Mr. Hogan left the room, and Ms. Tessier smiled at him. Ken offered up a smile back and saw for the first time she looked older than his father.

She pulled a chair close to him, sat down, and Ken caught sight of a small rectangular, white and pale blue pin on the left breast of her white shirt.

"How are you feeling, Ken?"

"I'm sore," he answered. "I hurt. May I ask you a question?"

"Of course," she smiled, picking up his right hand and looking at his skinned knuckles.

"Is that a Korean war ribbon?"

For a split second, she stiffened, and then she nodded. "How did you know?"

"I read a lot," Ken told her.

Ms. Tessier straightened up. "My children read a lot. None of them ever knew what this pin was. None of them asked. Let's get these cleaned up, alright?"

He nodded.

As she went about the office, looking for the supplies, Ms. Tessier asked, "What do you know about Korea, Ken?"

He frowned. "A little. It was fought from nineteen-fifty to nineteen-fifty-three. It's not officially a war, even though we had a lot of people killed. My father's friend, Bill, he was in Korea. He said he was part of the Chosin Frozen."

She glanced over her shoulder at Ken, and he saw her eyes were filled with sadness. "Then you know more than most. A lot more. Ah, here it is."

Ms. Tessier brought the supplies she had been looking for back to Ken and sat down once more.

"I was a nurse in the Army," she explained. "The fighting at Chosin had ended just a few days prior when I arrived in Korea. I was part of what was called a MASH unit. Do you know what they were?"

"Yes," Ken nodded, closed his eyes and said, "Mobile Army Surgical Hospital."

When he opened his eyes again, Ken saw Ms. Tessier smiling at him. "Yes. That's it exactly."

Ken returned the smile and held his hands out as she finished cleaning the cuts. He made sure not to wince as the alcohol stung the open wounds.

"So, do you read more than just military history?" Ms. Tessier asked.

Ken shook his head. "Not really. I mean, I've read a few books, classics, I guess? But no, it's mostly history."

A frown passed over her face. "Why?"

He shrugged. "I'm not sure. I guess because I need to be ready."

"Ready for what?"

"I have to be a soldier."

She stopped and looked at him closely. Then, in a soft, firm voice, she asked, "Who told you that?"

"No one," Ken answered.

"Then why do you think you have to be a soldier?"

"Because everyone in my family has been a soldier."

Ms. Tessier took a deep breath, and in the same tone, she spoke again. "Tell me who everyone is."

"My father," Ken told her. "He was in Vietnam. My grandfather, he was in World War Two. My great-grandfather fought in World War One. He was a German soldier. My father said we've always been soldiers. As far back as you go."

"What about your mother's side of the family?" Ms. Tessier asked.

"I don't know," Ken answered. "My mom left when I was about two. I don't know anyone on her side."

Ms. Tessier sat in silence for a moment. "Ken, terrible things happen to people in war."

"I know."

She raised an eyebrow. "Do you? War isn't all medals and glory. It's sadness and pain. Blood and death. It's things I never knew. It's, it's killing, Ken. And sometimes that's not the worst of it."

"I know," Ken whispered.

Ms. Tessier waited for him to continue, and so Ken did.

"Mr. Essex, who lives next door, he lost his legs in World War One. And both his brothers. My father's friend, Lee, his head is scarred. There's something wrong with him. In his brain now." Ken paused, then added, "And some of my father's friends, they seem really sad."

"What about your dad, Ken?" she asked. "Does he speak about Vietnam?"

Ken shook his head. "He doesn't ever. Sometimes, when I walk into the room, they'll be talking about it, but then they stop. He won't let them talk about it."

"He's in charge?"

Ken nodded.

Ms. Tessier took a deep breath and let it out slowly. "I'm going to tell you something, Ken. Something not even my children know, but that's because none of them ever talked about joining the Army. Or any other branch, for that matter. If they had, I would have told them. Are you listening?"

"Yes, ma'am."

"Good." She leaned closer, and Ken could smell lilacs. "I was nineteen when I went to Korea. Nineteen when I got to the MASH unit. I had to leave my bags on the truck because they were bringing wounded in. The Koreans were pushing toward us. It was bad. I'd never seen so much blood. So many people dying. I was trying to help a soldier. He was missing most of his face, Ken. It was gone."

Ms. Tessier closed her eyes and kept them closed as she continued.

"I had an arm around his waist, and I was holding his pistol. Then, the North Koreans were there. They were yelling and shooting and trying to get to the wounded. The soldier I was helping, he was hit again in the legs, and he fell down, pulling me with him. The

North Korean who shot him came running up, and I pulled the trigger, Ken."

Ms. Tessier opened her eyes, and there were tears of sadness and anger. "I killed the North Korean. I've thought of him a lot. Thought about what he made me do. All I wanted to be was a nurse, Ken. I wanted to help people. My brother, he had been wounded in World War Two, and he talked about how wonderful the nurses had been. I wanted to be that for someone else."

She took a tissue out of a nearby box and dabbed at her eyes. "I would be, later on. But that first day there, I was a killer. I was everything I didn't want to be. That's what war did to me, Ken. That's what being a soldier did. Because that's what I was, first and foremost. I was a soldier, and I couldn't let my wounded brother die."

Silence filled the small office.

Ken swallowed and whispered, "I'm sorry you had to kill someone."

Ms. Tessier nodded. "So am I. I didn't tell you to scare you, Ken. I told you so you would know what a soldier has to do. Even a soldier nurse. You don't have to be anything that you don't want to be, Ken. Please, understand that. You just have to be you."

"But what if I'm a soldier?" Ken asked. "What if that's what I am?"

Her smile was one of sadness and loss.

"Then that's what you are," she sighed. She reached out, picked up his hands and smiled again. "But I don't think so, Ken."

He nodded, closed his eyes, and wondered what it would be like to kill one man to save another.

COLONEL ESSEX'S KITCHEN

"You gonna be okay?"

Ken closed his book and looked up at his father. "Yes."

His father poured himself some coffee, sat down at the table and said, "You know I don't want to go, Kid."

"I know."

His father sipped at his drink. "I'll be gone for three days. You'll eat with the Cristos, and they'll check in on you. Where's the number for my hotel?"

"On the dresser," Ken answered.

His father nodded. "And extra money, if you need it?"

"In a can in the freezer."

His father smiled. "Good.

A horn beeped outside, and Ken's father sighed. They stood up together, and Ken waited as his father emptied his mug into the sink and rinsed it out before setting it on the drying rack. His father gave him a hug, kissed him on the forehead and said, "Be good, Kid. Your dad loves you."

"Love you, too."

His father smiled, picked up his suitcase and left the apartment.

Ken went to the window in the front room, looked down into the street, and saw his father appear a few moments later. A cab waited at the curb, and soon, his father was gone.

Ken listened to the apartment for a short time. The refrigerator hummed in the kitchen, and from the hallway came the muted squawks and cries of the Cristos' chickens. Ken slipped his hands into his pockets and felt the ten dollars his father had given him.

Ken smiled and turned away from the window. He went into the hall, pulled on his jacket and hat, and then left the apartment. When he reached the open door to the Cristos, he knocked and waited for a response.

Mr. Cristo appeared in the far doorway, buttoning up a dark blue uniform shirt. Over the left breast, in bright white cloth tape, was the name *A+ Cleaners*. In the same type of tape, and over his right breast, was his name, *Jean Claude*.

"Ken." Mr. Cristo smiled. "Is everything well?"

"Yes. I'm going next door to see Colonel Essex," Ken explained. "I might go to the bookstore after."

"As long as you are safe," Mr. Cristo replied, his smile faltering. "Be sure you pay attention when you walk, yes?"

Ken remembered Henri's death and nodded. "I will, Mr. Cristo."

"Good. Mama Cristo is making joumou for dinner."

Ken's stomach rumbled at the thought of the soup. Smiling, he told Mr. Cristo, "I'll be here."

"Good."

Ken waved goodbye and continued down the stairs to the porch. He buttoned up his jean jacket and walked around the back of the apartment building to the far left of the wall that separated the driveway from Colonel Essex's property. At the end of the wall, Ken clambered up and over it, brushed off his hands and then headed for Colonel Essex's backdoor. When he reached it, Ken knocked on the door and waited.

It took a few moments, but the door opened soon enough, and Mrs. Dunne, the colonel's occasional housekeeper, greeted him.

"Good morning, Ken." She smiled and held the door for him. "Is Mr. Essex expecting you?"

"No, ma'am," Ken answered.

"Well, take a seat, I'm sure he will be happy to see you."

Ken removed his hat and jacket, then hung them on the hooks by the back door. As she left the kitchen, Ken sat down at the small table. He heard a soft knock, then she spoke, her words low and unintelligible.

A creak followed, and then the familiar sound of Colonel Essex's wheelchair.

The older man smiled broadly as he rolled up to the table.

"To what do I owe this unexpected pleasure?" the man asked, locking the wheels into place.

"I was thinking of going to the bookstore, and I didn't know if you would like me to find anything new for you to read."

Colonel Essex raised a white eyebrow, his smile broadening into a grin. "You stopped by to see if I would like a book?"

Ken smiled and nodded. "My dad gave me some money. He's gone for a few days."

The man's grin faded slightly. "For a few days?"

"Yes. Three. The commander said he had to go and do some stuff at another base." Ken shrugged. "But it's okay. I'll be eating with the Cristos."

"Ah. The Haitian family of your friend?"

Ken nodded and tried not to think of Henri.

"I suspect they enjoy your company a bit?" Colonel Essex's voice was soft.

"Yeah," Ken murmured. "I like to visit with them. And Mama Cristo, she's a really good cook."

Colonel Essex looked at him for a moment. "Ken, would you mind if I asked you a personal question?"

Surprised, Ken shook his head. "No. I mean, I don't think I would."

"You don't have to answer it," the man continued. "I've been curious about your mother. Where is she?"

Ken shrugged. "She left when I was really young. I've asked my dad a few times, and he always says the

167

same thing. 'Took off, Kid. Got drunk, threw the keys at me and said have fun with your brat.'"

Colonel Essex winced as though struck. He took a deep breath and asked, "Have you ever heard from her again?"

"No," Ken answered. "My Aunt Mary, she sends me a birthday card every year, but she never talks about my mom. I don't think anybody knows where she is."

"Does it bother you not knowing?"

Ken considered the question for a moment. "No. Not really. I mean, I get sad every once in a while, like around Mother's Day, but that's about it. I figure if she wants to say hi, she will. She and my dad are still married, technically. He said it was cheaper than divorcing her."

Ken looked down at his hands and was surprised to see he was squeezing them.

"If you ever decide you would like to look for your mother," Colonel Essex said, "and if I am in any way able to assist, I would be more than happy to, Ken."

"Thanks." Ken smiled. "So, do you want anything at the bookstore?"

Colonel Essex chuckled. "No. I don't believe that I do. If, however, you see something you think I would be interested in, then, by all means, purchase it. I would be most happy to read it upon your recommendation."

"Okay." Ken got to his feet.

"And when you return from your adventure," the man continued, "stop here for a cup of tea and some cake. Mrs. Dunne brought a wonderful cake with her today, and I will make myself ill should I eat it all."

Ken laughed. "Okay, sir."

He put on his jacket and hat, and when he waved goodbye, there was sadness in the old man's eyes.

"I will see you shortly, Mr. Gunther," the colonel stated, "and I hope you will be well-armed with new books."

"Me too," Ken grinned and left the warmth of the kitchen.

CHIEF PETTY OFFICER OSIPYAN

The bell above the door rang and welcomed Ken into the bookstore.

When he stepped across the threshold and the door closed behind him, Ken paused, enjoying the smell of the books around him. Some had the faint, crisp odor of new paper and fresh ink. Tight bindings and old ideas wrapped in new words.

These thoughts drifted at the edges of Ken's consciousness. They were pushed aside and relegated to their place by the powerful smell of old books.

Ken took a deep breath, the scent of age enveloping him. He could picture Colonel Essex's parlor and the books lining the shelves. His fingers tingled with the memory of the leather binding of *Treasure Island* and the weight of *Moby Dick*.

A thump sounded and brought Ken back to reality, as did the sudden grumble of a man.

"Ah, cock it!"

An old man limped into view at the far end of the store, and there was another thump as he dropped a hammer onto the top of the desk.

The man looked up, saw Ken, and then sighed and flashed a rueful smile. "Ah hell, son, didn't see you there. Sorry about the language."

"That's okay, sir," Ken replied.

The old man's eyebrow went up. "Huh. Polite. I like that. Come on down, come on down. Name's Serj, Serj Osipyan. My boy, Alex, he owns this store. Daughter-in-law's currently giving birth to twins, so, you know, he's there with her."

Ken walked down the center aisle and came to a stop in front of the desk as Serj settled into the chair.

"Ah, Christ, my damned knees hurt today," the old man sighed. "You a reader?"

"Yes, sir."

Serj chuckled. "So's my boy, Alex. Guess he's not a boy, though, huh? He's thirty-three now."

Ken nodded his head and smiled in agreement.

"So, what do you like to read?" Serj asked.

"Mostly military books, sir," Ken answered.

"Huh. Alex did, too, when he was your age. Decided to join the Navy like his old man. Life was good for him, though. Shellback, you know?"

Ken shook his head.

"You read about the military, and you don't know what a shellback is?" the old man teased.

"No," Ken smiled. "My father was in the Army."

"Ah." The old man scratched at the back of his head. "Well, a shellback is a sailor on the surface. Destroyers, battleships, aircraft carriers, the whole works."

"Oh. Well, my Dad works for the Navy, though," Ken added.

"Oh yeah? Where at?"

"At the Groton Sub Base," Ken answered.

"Ah, that's where I finished out my time," Serj stated. "That's how we ended up here. What's your dad's name? I might know him."

"Mike Gunther," Ken said. "He works with the scrappies."

Serj laughed. "Oh, I know, Mike. He's a good guy. Hell, you must be Ken, then. Your dad talks about you all the time. Got your picture on the desk and everything. Glad to meet you, Ken."

The old man leaned over the desk and offered his hand.

Ken shook it, trying not to look at the strange smoothness of the man's hand and the lack of fingernails. The hand was almost like a cartoon drawing.

"Yeah," Serj nodded, withdrawing his hand after having shaken Ken's. "Both are like that."

He held up both hands and waggled his fingers at Ken. "Bad luck back in forty-five."

"What happened in nineteen-forty-five, sir?"

"Japs happened," the man replied. "I was on the *USS Franklin* when she got hit. March second, nineteen-forty-five. Bad day, Ken. Terrible day. I was burned. Not as bad as some, you see. But pretty bad. Hell of a day. Lost a few friends."

Serj tapped on the top of the desk with his smooth fingers. He smiled at Ken. "Your father says you remember a lot. That true?"

"Yes, sir."

The smile faded from the old man's face. He cleared his throat. "Those were some of the worst hours of my life, Ken."

Ken remained silent and listened.

Serj looked at his hands. "They weren't that bad, you know. Not at first. It wasn't until after we found him. Bobby Doyle. He was my shipmate. We'd gone through training together, and then both got duty aboard the *Franklin*. We used to talk about what we'd do after the war, of course. I'd tell him about wanting to stay in, and he'd talk about how he wanted to open a garage. He was great with machines. Kind of guy who could put his ear up against an engine and tell you what was wrong with it. When he was off duty, Bobby would go down to the machine shop and play around. Pull stuff apart or fabricate something. Just a good guy."

Serj cleared his throat again and looked up at the ceiling, wiping something away from his eye. When he spoke, his voice was rougher.

"I found Bobby on fire," the old man stated. "Terrible. He was covered in oil and just burning. I tried to slap the flames out, but they just wouldn't go out. Too much oil. The chaplain was there. Good man. He tried to help me put the fire out, but it wouldn't.

Bobby was screaming. Just screaming about wanting to die. He wanted someone to kill him. The chaplain, he was a Catholic priest, and he said some stuff in Latin to Bobby, and then, to me, he goes, 'It's okay.'"

Serj looked at Ken, his eyes rimmed red and filled with tears. "He told me it was okay. My hands were pretty bad at that point, and Bobby was still burning, but I put my hands over his nose and mouth."

Serj stopped and put his head in his hands. For a moment, his shoulders heaved, and it sounded as though he were coughing. Ken stood at the desk, unsure of what to do, his stomach twisting and churning.

After a minute, Serj wiped his eyes and straightened up. He looked at Ken, and sadness hung about the man.

"Will you remember that for me, Ken?" Serj asked.

"Bobby Doyle," Ken whispered, "and the *Franklin*. The chaplain said it was okay."

"Yes," Serj sighed. "The chaplain said it was okay."

Ken stood there, and he remembered.

MIDNIGHT AND WHISPERS

The phone rang.

A short, sharp burst jarred Ken from sleep.

He sat up and looked around as the phone stopped. Before it could ring again, Ken's father answered the phone. The light from the kitchen spilled into the hallway, and Ken could see his father's shadow, the coiled cord of the phone connecting him to the wall.

"Who the fuck is this?"

The anger and slurring of the words told Ken his father was drunk, not on beer but whiskey.

"You got a lot of fuckin' nerve callin' here," his father snarled.

There was a pause, and Ken wondered who was on the other end.

"Yeah, you know what, don't care if you found God." His father let out a bitter laugh. "Ain't nothin' to me, ain't nothin' to my son."

The pause was shorter as his father cut someone off.

"Nope, he ain't yours, Winnie," his father growled. "You gave him up. No...no, you listen to me, you stuck-up little bitch, this ain't about me. This is about him. This is about...about my boy. I'm here. I'm raisin' him. You ain't. You understand?"

A long silence followed, and if his father's shadow wasn't still in the doorway, Ken would have thought the call had ended.

"'Course you knew I was goin' be up," his father laughed. "I haven't slept the night since sixty-seven. And why are you callin' anyway, huh? Oh, you got permission. Uh huh, two-thirty and, what? Oh, big fuckin' deal, Winnie. So it's eleven-thirty in god-damned California. Yeah, so what if I'm drinkin'? Yeah? Really? You know why it doesn't matter, Winifred, because I am here with my son. Where are you? Where've you been?"

Ken's father laughed again, a sound filled with anger and bitterness.

"A convent? That's rich, Winnie. That's really great. You really did find God, huh?" Ken saw his father's shadow shake its head. "No, I don't care if you are a goddamned nun. You ain't seein' my boy. No…No, I ain't goin' say he's yours because you gave that up, Winnie. You gave up that right, and you don't ever get to forget it. Never."

A silence followed, and Ken's father lowered his head. "Really, Winnie? You want me to put the boy on the phone and have him talk to you? Yeah, I'm sure he's awake too. Fuckin' phone ringin' at two-thirty in the morning, bound to wake the dead. Pretty sure he's listenin' in too. So what? You want me to stroll in there and go, hey, Kid, get up and talk to your mom. She's found God and wants to talk to you. Fuck you. Fuck that. You ain't goin' to get to say that unless you come in person…I don't care if you live in California now and you can't! He's here, Winnie! He's here, and he's the best-goddamned kid that's ever walked the face of this fuckin' planet! There has never, in the history of boys, been a better boy than him, and you threw that right the fuck out the window because you wanted to party and put shit up your nose. Fuck you."

His father let out a deep laugh, and when he spoke, the anger was gone from his voice. "Who are you kidding, Winnie? I got over you. I don't miss you. I don't love you. You lost all of that when you left our son. Christ, Winnie, this isn't about you. You can't get that, huh? You can't understand this is about Ken. Everything. Absolutely everything is about Ken. I work my ass off for that boy. I put money in the fucking bank for him. I don't date 'cause I don't want to be away from him any more than I have to, and I don't want anybody messin' with our time."

There was silence as Ken's father's shadow moved away from the door.

"No," his father continued. "Nope. You can't talk to him. I got friends who are lawyers now, Winnie. Officers at the base. Hell, I know the commander would go to bat for me. I do good work, but more important, they know Ken, Winnie. They have more of a relationship with my son than you ever will."

Ken heard the whiskey bottle open and the liquor poured into a glass.

"Listen," his father snapped. "Just because you gave birth to him doesn't make you his mother. The fuckin' Haitian neighbors love him more than you do. That boy is loved, Winnie, just not by you. You were his mother, and you threw that shit away."

His father paused. "Oh, fuck you. No, nope. I don't care if you cry, Winnie. I don't. You're not going to call here again. Especially not at this time of night. You want to talk to my son, then we can go to court, and we'll hammer that shit out. Yup...yup... that's right, Winnie. Court. Have your Mother Superior or the Pope or who the fuck ever get a lawyer so you can see my son."

Ken's father hung up the phone and turned the light out in the kitchen. Ken listened as the man walked down to the front room, and then the chair groaned as his father sat down in the dark.

Ken tried to close his eyes and go back to sleep, but his mind wouldn't let him. He thought about his mother, and he wondered if he looked like her. There were no pictures of her in the apartment. Nothing at all. Ken had asked one day, and his father had said he'd thrown them all out after a couple of years.

After Ken's mother hadn't returned and his father had given up hope that she would.

Pressure on Ken's bladder finally made him cast aside the blankets and get up. He walked quietly to the bathroom, went in, relieved himself and washed up. When he finished, he peaked in at his father, who sat with his eyes closed in the near darkness of the room.

One eye opened halfway.

"You good?" his father mumbled.

"No," Ken replied.

"Come on." His father patted his lap, and Ken went in, curled up on his father's lap and waited as the man picked up an old brown and yellow afghan, draping it over them both. "You heard it all?"

"Yes."

"Mm."

Ken closed his eyes and rested his head against his father's broad chest, listening to the man's steady heartbeat.

"She knew I'd be awake," his father murmured.

Ken listened.

"Had the same dream for years," his father continued, his voice rising and falling with his chest. "I'm in the Huey. We're coming in, weapons hot. I've got the sixty and just chewing up the paddy. Charlie's there, all over the place. He's got an ARVN unit, a special forces team and a mike team pinned down. We don't do runs like this. Strictly search and destroy, Kid."

His father's voice became softer.

"But this, this was an all-call. We needed to get them out. Captain brings the bird in low, skids just over the paddy. Team starts loading the wounded on. Special forces guys, they're there with the mikes, providing security while the ARVN unit is supposed to keep Charlie back. Least long enough for the wounded to get out. But they don't. They break, the little yellow fuckers."

His father's heart thumped wildly, and his voice became strained.

"In reality, Kid," his father whispered, "we got the wounded on board. The ARVN fuckers, they grabbed onto the skids. I kicked 'em off. Broke jaws, crushed hands, kicked teeth in. Didn't matter. I had a grease gun, and I put a few rounds into the fucks too. Wounded needed to get out. But my dream, Kid, in my dream, there's too many of 'em."

Ken felt his father's muscles tighten, and the words were bitten off.

"They drag us down into the paddy," his father hissed, "and we all die. Every fuckin' one of us."

His father took a long, shuddering breath. "Every night, I look for my rifle. 'Cause I got to put the barrel in my mouth and pull the trigger. I ain't goin' to be taken alive. Not by them. I know what they do."

His father wrapped his arms around Ken and held onto him.

"Every night," his father whispered, "I need to find my rifle."

DISCUSSION QUESTIONS

1. Describe Ken. What does he look like to you? What does he like to do? What kind of person is he?

2. What is Ken's relationship with his father? Are there other adults in his life who are important to him?

3. How does Colonel Essex influence Ken? Is this influence good or bad?

4. Would you describe Ken as a normal child? Does he have a lot of friends?

5. Who are Ken's neighbors in the apartment building? Are they important in his life? Is he important to them?

6. Ken spends the majority of his time surrounded by men. How might this affect his relationship with other children? How might it affect his interactions with adults?

7. Why does Ken listen? How do you think he acquired the skill to listen to people and not just hear their words?

8. Books are an important part of Ken's life. Why do you think this is? How do they affect him?

9. What is it that Ken thinks he is required to do? How does this shape who he is and how he acts?

10. When his mother calls late at night, how do you think his father's reaction affects Ken?

"A TRUE WAR STORY"

For most of us who write about war and the military, I believe Tim O'Brien is our Pied Piper. He leads us, dancing, down a dangerous path with a song we can't break away from, one that has us searching for truth where no truth necessarily exists.

There is a beautiful, powerful quote, one of many, from his book *The Things They Carried*. In it, O'Brien clearly states that a true war story is never about war.

That's what I hope to have captured here. These war stories are not about war. They are, as O'Brien has defined them, about the violence and the obscenity of war. How do they affect the men and women who have partaken in war? How does this affect their families?

When I first set out to write these stories, I titled the collection *Killers in Their Youth*, and it was only going to be stories about combat. Then, I realized how narrow that idea was and how much it limited not only the experiences of those veterans I have met with but our own understanding of war through their experiences.

I can remember, when I was eight or nine years old, asking my father about his time in Vietnam. His reply had been sharp, sharper than he had intended.

"I did three years in Germany before Vietnam. There's a hell of a lot more to the Army than killing."

This statement by my father, spoken some 40 years ago, has stayed with me. It made me think about the stories I've heard and the men and women who have shared them with me.

Yes, there's killing, and there's death in the stories I've written here. They are, after all, war stories. But there's more to them than that. There's the violence and the hatred, the rage and the bitterness that is often the byproduct of war and violence. Some of this is directed at others; some is focused inward.

As I said at the beginning, these are a fine mixture of truth and fiction. They are true war stories, and by that, they aren't necessarily the whole truth at all.

When I was a young boy, my father trained me to hear history.

I grew up listening to men speak of death, mostly when they thought I wasn't paying attention.

They didn't try to shield me from violence. They just didn't want to share the stories with me. Their stories, their history, was just that – it was theirs. They were Soldiers and Marines, Sailors and Airmen, Coasties and Merchant Marines. Most of them were hard-fighting men in their youth.

When I met them, they were no longer young. The oldest of them were in their late '70s and early '80s. Friends and coworkers of my father, men who lived in and around us in small rooms on narrow streets. They'd fought in World War One, and they'd seen a side of war no one had known previously. It was wholesale slaughter, miles of land turned into a mass-ive abattoir. More than a few had served in World War Two, and they'd fought in every theater and in every place imaginable.

Here and there were some veterans of Korea, men and women who had left and returned home with none of their friends or family members being the wiser.

Most of the men I met had served in Vietnam. They were my father's friends.

Most of what you read was true. And when I say most of it, it's the essentials, the bones and the marrow.

Names are changed, but the stories are true. Word for word truth?

No, of course not.

Most of these stories were told when I was a young boy, more than 30 years ago. Most of these men and women are dead. Cancer, suicide, and murder, to name a few.

I can see them, though. I can remember them. Where they were sitting, where they were standing. Mannerisms and quirks. Men who scratched at old wounds, who peered into the past and could see the war as though it stood waiting for them in the next room. I can remember twitching fingers and jittery legs, endless cigarettes smoked and years lost to darkness.

I'll get some details wrong, and I won't even worry about the names.

Because in the end, those don't matter. Their stories do. Their stories tell the history of generations.

DEAD RECKONING COLLECTIVE is a veteran owned and operated publishing company. Our mission encourages literacy as a component of a positive lifestyle. Although DRC only publishes the written work of military veterans, the intention of closing the divide between civilians and veterans is held in the highest regard. By sharing these stories it is our hope that we can help to clarify how veterans should be viewed by the public and how veterans should view themselves.

Visit us at:

deadreckoningco.com

@deadreckoningcollective

@deadreckoningco

@DRCpublishing